A PARABLE

and a

WARNING

Michael O'Sheasy

ISBN 978-1-63961-678-7 (paperback)
ISBN 978-1-63961-995-5 (hardcover)
ISBN 978-1-63961-679-4 (digital)

Christian Faith Publishing
832 Park Avenue
Meadville, PA 16335
www.christianfaithpublishing.com

Printed in the United States of America

As the author of this story, I hope you find it entertaining. My grand-daughter, Lila, asked me—her Beebop—if she could be in the book, and so Lila is until the very end. I dedicate this book to Lila and her three brothers: Caleb, Ethan, and Dylan.

PROLOGUE

This story, which I told to my granddaughter Lila, is about the lives of three marooned families based upon a message found in a bottle washed up onto the beach at Año Nuevo (better known for its elephant seals) in Northern California.

Mankind has been placing messages in bottles for hundreds of years, some for fun, some for rescue, some even for mapping the currents of the oceans. Some have floated around the oceans for decades. In the eighteenth century, a seaman from Japan shipwrecked on a South Pacific island placed a message in a bottle and flung it out around 1794 into the ocean. It was found in 1935, washed up on a Japanese shore. The message from our marooned islanders appears to simply tell what has happened to them. This parable is based upon the bizarre *message in a bottle*, and the warning pertains to concerns about our country's future.

Apparently, our marooned islanders came up with a sustainable survival plan but, after some years of sacrifice to maintain the plan, are considering a modification or even abandonment of the plan. This could enable greater food (resource) availability today yet create a deficit for tomorrow's food (resource) needs and consequential islanders' suffering.

At the same time back home, our government in America is printing cash at an alarming rate. Our deficit is rapidly expanding; this deficit is financed by debt (i.e., bonds) that eventually must be paid back via increased tax revenue. One can view this spending today and paying back tomorrow along with increased money supply as an attempt to kick-start a moribund economy. The assumed goal that these efforts today will enable are benefits greater than the negative impacts of increased inflation plus forgone benefits from innovations and productivity gains that would have otherwise occurred in the absence of a stimulus and subsequent tax increases. Are we as a country on a road to collapse as these marooned islanders may be?

Any irony or humor has been retained in order to match, as well as possible, that of the message in the bottle. The story is chock-full of metaphors. So there, you have been dutifully warned.

CHAPTER 1

A Cruise

The year is 2024 long after the nightmare of 2020–2021 with its coronavirus pandemic and hybrids. Life had returned to normal although memories lingered especially for those many families who had lost loved ones. The precoronavirus Gross Domestic Product (GDP) of the United States was back, and the economy was roaring once again. Cruise ships were full, and new ships under construction.

A new cruise ship, *A Time to Remember*, of NCL lineage had left its port of Los Angeles sailing to the South Pacific with eight thousand passengers onboard for a four-week cruise. However, after the sixth day and two ports of calls, members of three families—Whitehead, Fernandez, and Cumberland—have become violently ill with symptoms frighteningly symptomatic of COVID-19—dry cough, sore throat, and fever of 103 degrees. The three families were quickly quarantined. The fact that there had not been a case of a coronavirus identified for twelve months anywhere in the world appeased few, if any, of the passengers. The captain tried to assuage everyone by explaining that appropriate precautions had taken place: quarantine was in place as was care and treatment for the three sick families, the ship had been completely detoxed, and authorities in the States had been notified. The ship was ordered by authorities to steam to its ultimate destination, the port of Sydney, Australia, with an ETA of six more days.

A couple of days later, two of the three children of the Whitehead family also became violently ill with said-same symptoms matching those of their infected father. Mrs. Fernandez continued experiencing symptoms, and one of the daughters of the Cumberland family had become worse. In spite of the captain's efforts to maintain the silence of the three families' conditions, word of the worsening virus spread quickly through the remaining 7,987 passengers. A "vigilante" group was formed to discover who might have been in contact with these three families (i.e., assigned seating for meals, tickets purchased for shows since sailing, friends who might have been on board, and even names of other passengers who were from the same cities in the States). This simply fed the flames of fear onboard.

A general meeting of only passengers was called, and a demand to the captain was issued for the ship to be sailed immediately toward any closer port than Sydney where the three families could be deposited. Unfortunately, the captain had to inform them that there were none. On the ninth day, near-panic reigned and order was almost nonexistent. An abnormal and growing number of passengers checked into sickbay feeling sickly although the medical staff found none of them testing positive for the virus.

The captain was alerted that the ship would soon run out of COVID-19 virus test kits. Fearing mutiny or simply civil disorder, the captain's first lieutenant alerted the captain that they would pass the next day by a small deserted island, about ninety acres in size, where the passengers could be off-loaded until authorities from Australia could subsequently rescue the three families. The first lieutenant added, "Captain, I know you don't want to leave the families there. Plus, you know, you'll get a lot of blowbacks from their families back home, but you don't have much choice if you want to avoid a possible mutiny and perhaps avoid further transmission of the virus. Captain, the three families are made up of a Hispanic family, an African American family, and a White family."

"That's about the only good thing I've heard. We shouldn't get any racist allegations," whispered the captain.

The captain determined that this would be an extreme but necessary solution to the impending disorder on the ship. Food, liquids, medical supplies, and sleeping bags would be left for the interment on the island.

The Fernandez, Cumberland, and Whitehead families were escorted onto the island with assurance that authorities would be notified immediately for rescue, and the cruise ship steamed away for Sydney.

*****

Now, as commonly known, the South Pacific is quite large, about the size of North America. Today's advanced technology enables precise tracking of ships throughout a cruise and for all weather conditions known to mankind. However, somewhat like the unexpected events of the coronavirus of 2020 that were also never previously known to mankind, another inexplicable event occurred this time on the sun at the exact time that the ship was transmitting its SOS message to Sydney.

A sunspot of only once-before-observed proportions was occurring sending a solar coronal mass ejection into the earth's atmosphere, producing a huge geomagnetic storm. In 1859, a powerful geomagnetic storm during a solar cycle occurred in the Earth's magnetosphere and created the largest geomagnetic storm on record. This storm, called the Carrington Event, caused serious damage to telegraph systems and today would have caused blackouts and extended outages of the electrical grid. Unlike the Carrington Event, this geomagnetic storm was most intense in the sparsely populated South Pacific because of this particular season of the year in the southern hemisphere. The ship's computers were fried, and the signaling of the ship's position was lost. The ship, however, was able to use nighttime navigational tools and dead reckoning during daylight hours which all pilots are still required to learn. And so *A Time to Remember* limped, they thought, toward Sydney.

CHAPTER 2

Marooned

As this was our first day on the island, it was now time to become better acquainted, and I shall begin narrating the story and describing our new island homes and cast of characters (and I do mean *characters*). None of us had any idea how long before rescue although we all figured it to be at least a week. (Did we ever underestimate!)

The three families found themselves as follows: the Whitehead father was named Clevis Whitehead from a long line of Whiteheads in Bayou La Batre, Alabama. You may not be familiar with Bayou La Batre, but it was made famous among major shrimping ports when shrimpers there discovered a most delectable shrimp called Royal Reds residing in about two hundred fathoms of water off its bay. The Whiteheads regularly attended the Pentecostal Baptist Church of Bayou La Batre.

Clevis introduced his family composed of his loving wife, Cornucopia (nicknamed Corny for more than one reason), and three boys. I am the oldest, have the strange name of Parrothead, and thankfully am called Parry. It seems that my mother and father were big fans of Jimmy Buffet when they were cavorting, accompanied by a drug habit Pa had picked up while in Vietnam. My parents quit the drug habit long before I came along, so my guess is that it was primarily recreational drugs like grass although it may have included some serious experimenting, possibly with LSD when you consider their naming convention for us boys. My two brothers are Pinhead (later they thankfully shortened it to PD) and Rufus. When my next oldest brother came along, the only thing my folks could think of close to Parrothead was Pinhead. No one in the family seems to recall how Rufus got his name, but Corny asserted that Rufus Whitehead sounded much better than had been their earlier inspiration for my second brother of Pinhead Whitehead.

Despite being raised on a farm, I enjoy reading a lot and am quite good at what locals refer to as "book-learning." I might have taken after my father, as he's inherently bright and could fool you with the not-so-uncommon misperception of a farmer.

I had wanted to go to Georgia Tech and walk on their football team, but I'm not good enough in math. In the fall, I'll be a junior at Tulane University with a double major in marine biology and history. When asked why I selected these two disparate majors, I tell them I simply want to know how old the oyster is that I'm eating.

Clevis, along with two of his three children, was infected with the coronavirus.

The Fernandez family were longtime friends of the Whiteheads. It turns out that Bobby Fernandez and Clevis were in marine boot camp together at Parris Island and became lifelong friends with both families oftentimes vacationing together in the Florida Keys. Bobby is a first-generation citizen of the United States, having been born in Miami after his mother and father escaped from Cuba. They are staunch Roman Catholics and attended Our Lady of the Lakes Roman Catholic Church in Miami Lakes. They have one son, Jesse, who is fifteen, and one daughter, Karmaranda, who is fourteen and nicknamed Karma. Karma has indeed brought her parents' good fortune (at least until they landed on this island), as Bobby had become highly successful running a lunch wagon (lightheartedly referred to as a roach coach) for the industrial businesses in the Palmetto Industrial Park of Miami.

Bobby's wife, Maria, was also the daughter of Cuban immigrants. Yet she has never learned to speak English in spite of being born in Miami. Not speaking English, however, never prevented her from being a very joyous, friendly person to all, even with those unable to speak her native language. She also was a remarkable cook.

You feel ravenous the very moment you enter their beautiful home with its tantalizing aromas emitted from the kitchen.

Bobby and Pa would take us three boys and Jesse to fish in Florida on shoreline reefs for grouper, lane snapper, hogfish, mangrove snapper, red snapper, yellowtail, red drum, triggerfish, pompano, sheepshead, barracuda (don't eat 'em, but are mighty fun to catch), crevalle jack (don't eat 'em, but are amazing to catch with their remarkable speed in the water), and some sea trout. When we weren't fishing or lobstering, we'd snorkel or scuba dive on the reefs, especially Pennekamp State Park.

Bobby and Pa would go out fishing in the ocean on Bobby's boat into the northward drifting Gulf stream where they'd usually catch mahi-mahi, permit, wahoo, Spanish mackerel, amberjack, kingfish, and cobia. They'd sometimes hook shark so big they'd pull Bobby's eighteen-foot boat until the shark would finally tire out. Bobby would then remove the hook, freeing the exhausted shark. They'd often fish at night, and one time, the small boat powered by a twenty-five-horsepower Evinrude engine broke down; the two fishermen had to spend the night drifting northward in the Gulf stream until daylight when they flagged down a larger fishing vessel that towed them back into the docks at Marathon where their wives waited fearfully and angrily. Come to think of it, that may have been the reason for the cruise that ended up getting us here.

We Whiteheads and the Fernandez family knew the Cumberlands from sharing the same dinner table together, which I'll tell you more about later. The Cumberland family was from what we in Alabama refer to as the "Left Coast" (San Francisco). The mother named Billie, along with her daughter Katelyn, was sick with the virus while the other daughter named Mischievous (nicknamed Missy, thank goodness) had no symptoms of coronavirus.

We would learn later that both Katelyn and Missy were excellent students in school, and fortunately for us, they brought along with them some of their schoolwork, pens, pencils, and writing paper. It seems Katelyn planned on writing some first drafts of college applications while on the cruise. Missy was getting ahead of her forthcoming English class by reading and writing synopses of classic novels:

Tolstoy's *Anna Karenina*, *Grapes of Wrath* by John Steinbeck, and *Les Misérables* by Victor Hugo. That was about all we knew about them when we first landed on the island, but we would later learn much more, especially my fondness for Katelyn. It'd soon be apparent that Mr. Cumberland while being a really nice person, had a tendency to be a little too full of himself.

Mr. Cumberland's first words to us were, "Since you folks don't know too much about us, let me add a little more background. My side of the family has been Jewish for some time, which is why I was named Jacob. Billie is a Jewish convert and attends the synagogue more regularly than I do because of my demanding job as a busy lawyer in the city. I'm summa cum laude from Berkeley." It would later become obvious that although Jacob often speaks of his intelligence, he knows that Billie is the real exceptional brain in the family.

Jacob next asserted, "I imagine you folks are thinking that *Jacob* is a common biblical name although you may not know that the original Jacob is regarded as a patriarch of the Israelites and is an important figure in all Abrahamic religions, such as Judaism, Christianity, and Islam. His grandfather, Abraham, was father to Isaac and Ishmael. Jacob was the second-born of Isaac's children, the elder being his fraternal twin brother, Esau. However, by deceiving Isaac when he was old and blind, Jacob was able to usurp the blessing that belonged to Esau as the firstborn son and became the leader of their family. Following a severe drought in his homeland of Canaan, Jacob and his descendants with the help of his son, Joseph, who had previously become a confidante of Pharaoh, settled in Egypt. There Jacob died, aged 147 years, and was buried in the Cave of Machpelah."

My brother Pinhead had had about enough of Jacob Cumberland pontificating on his Jewish knowledge and tersely asked, "Where does the name *Billie* show up in the Bible?"

"Well, I'm glad you asked. It's not directly from the Bible, yet it's something that I'm sure my wife would like to inform you of."

"Hush, Jacob, no one wants to hear any more about our family names," responded Billie.

"Yes, I would," retorted Pinhead.

"Well, if you won't tell them, Billie, I will," declared Jacob. "Our Billie was named for the famous Black singer Billie Holiday, a distant relative who was probably the greatest jazz and blues singer of her era in spite of having a difficult life. Ms. Holiday had a unique sultry, mellow, yet melancholic voice. She performed in clubs in the thirties and late forties along with other famous names you might recall, Louis Armstrong, Bessie Smith, Gene Krupa, Benny Goodman, and Count Basie. Two of her most renowned songs are 'God Bless the Child' and 'Strange Fruit.' She was way ahead of her time in recognizing and exposing the hardships of African Americans. For example, she sang 'Strange Fruit' sixteen years before Rosa Parks refused to give up her seat on a Montgomery, Alabama, bus. 'Strange Fruit' was actually a protest song about the horrible lynching of Blacks in America. When Billie would sing the song in nightclubs, the predominant White audiences would either clap their hands until sore or walk out.

"Ms. Holiday achieved her fame despite her background. She was born into poverty-stricken teenagers. Clarence Holiday was only fifteen, and Sadie Fagan was only thirteen. Later, as life continued its hardships, Billie and her mother turned to prostitution. Billie ended up in prison for a short while. After release, she tried to get a job as a dancer in a nightclub, was turned down, but offered a job to sing for $2 per night. This led to linking up with Benny Goodman, and she catapulted there to fame.

"However, racism would continue to haunt her. Her father died at age thirty-nine after being denied treatment at a Whites-only hospital. While performing in the South, she would often be banned from sitting with White vocalists and was asked to use the hotel's freight elevator instead of the passenger elevator for Whites. Billie turned to heroin and was arrested for a narcotics violation in 1947. Her later life was fraught with abusive men along with drug and alcohol excess.

"In 1959, she was arrested for drug possession and soon died of pulmonary edema and heart failure at New York's Metropolitan Hospital. She was forty-four years old and had seventy cents in her bank account. Despite her life's hardship, her enduring legacy lives

8

on, including a Lifetime Achievement Grammy hall of fame and the Rock and Roll Hall of Fame. We are very proud of who my wife was named for," exclaimed Jacob.

"Enough about my namesake and introductions. This is just our first day on the island, and we'll have plenty of time to get to know each other better in the days to come. Let's figure what kind of living habitat that has been forced upon us," submitted Billie.

The remainder of day one for the three families followed with some exploring of the island, which encompassed approximately ninety acres all with beachfront access. Mr. Cumberland, Mr. Fernandez, and Mrs. Whitehead—the three adults who had not been infected—began building, as best they could, a lean-to using flotsam found on the beach along with the tent provisions "generously" provided by the ship within which the three families could shelter when necessary until rescue.

That afternoon, a brief tropical rain shower occurred, comforting all with the awareness that freshwater should be regularly available until rescue. With optimism abundant, Missy laughed. "You know, we've got in our provisions several empty bottles into which we can write messages to hopefully communicate with the outside world."

Food provided by the ship would suffice for several weeks, and to everyone's pleasant surprise, there was plenty of fruit, including bananas, Malay apples, swamp taro, breadfruit, sugarcane for sugarcane juice, coconut, and candlenut trees. Mrs. Whitehead, being a farmer's wife, proclaimed that the land was easily cleared, and the rich topsoil on the island was probably capable of farming "although there should be little need for this with the pending rescue."

On day two, Mrs. Whitehead's oldest son, Pinhead, discovered in his sleeping bag that a cruel and senseless joke had been played upon him by his new worst friend from the cruise ship: a boy named Judus. He had placed in Pinhead's sleeping bag a container of various garden vegetable seeds along with a note reading, "Don't plan on a rescue anytime soon, Jughead, but here's a way to survive." (It was never known why Judus had such a bag of seeds on the cruise ship.) Clevis offered a little comfort that a likely rescue made garden vegetable seeds of insignificant value and that their placement reflected a warped, sick mind. Little did the island dwellers know what had happened on the ship.

*****

On *A Time to Remember*, the loss of the ship's computers due to the enormous sunspot, along with the captain's and pilot's conflicting opinions on the passenger ship's actual sailing coordinates, led to the ship sailing off course. The ship ended up missing Sydney by seven hundred miles and finally docked in Brisbane. Authorities were notified in both Australia and the United States. This lack of communication for the ship after off-loading us onto the deserted island, loss of electronic files for the ship's navigational course, and confusion over actual coordinates would make rescue attempts extremely difficult, as search parties began for what was comically termed Gilligan's Island for a reason known only to baby boomers.

Countries from around the world joined in the search to no avail. A psychic in San Francisco revealed that she had envisioned some of the family members flying aboard the missing airliner from Kuala Lumpur, Malaysia, although there had been no subsequent landing of the airplane. Search-and-rescue attempts would eventually cease after twelve months. The three families were never found despite the extensive search effort.

*****

Days three through twenty-two on the island included everyone's complete recovery from the virus. We discovered an extinct volcano with a crater near the middle of the island and at an elevation of about ten feet. The crater itself was about two hundred feet across and had contained a beautiful freshwater pond fed daily by the afternoon tropical showers. We decided to build another lean-to inside the cavern in anticipation of possible storms. We positioned the lean-to toward the west where most winds seem to originate. We slanted the roof, with the low end in the direction of a likely storm, and buried the low end about six inches into the ground.

Surrounding the crater was lava rock and, of great surprise, hard rocks that Mr. Cumberland identified as basalt which he claimed could be used to make adzes (an ancient cutting tool similar to an ax) and obsidian glass for making cutting utensils. The island proved to be home to numerous colonies of birds as a possible source of meat for us. Many were flightless or simply weak fliers or could be captured on their nests. We identified petrels, sandpipers, terns, tropicbirds, and flightless pigeons.

We delighted in learning that we boys could catch some modest-sized fish and shellfish to eat, and much of the fruit was delicious. It became quickly apparent that there would be a need to cook the fish, and therefore, a fire would be necessary as it would also for warmth on some cool, windy nights. No one had carried along matches, and there were no convenience stores on the island. However, Pinhead was a periodic weed (pot) smoker back home in Bayou La Batre and had brought a cigarette lighter in his luggage.

This would solve the pending problem of igniting a fire, but what if the fluid in the lighter were to ever be consumed prior to rescue? Mr. Cumberland asserted that it would be best for the families to maintain a fire burning 24-7 for that possibility, which satisfied the group. Between the deadwood on the island and driftwood that floated up, there should be ample fuel, plus the smoke from the fire might attract search parties. We also began using mollusk shells for chopping, dippers, spoons, and spades. *We were beginning to become Swiss Family Robinson*, we thought!

However, this all was of little consolation to the growing despair that maybe the three families wouldn't get rescued, or at least for some time. A source of a positive note was the recovery of Clevis and his infected sons, now healthy, and recovery of Corny and Mrs. Cumberland and her daughter, Katelyn, as well as Mrs. Fernandez. No one else seemed to have been stricken by the deadly virus.

CHAPTER 3

Government

Day twenty-three called for a democratic meeting of all members currently residing on the island to discuss planning for a future void of rescue. The first to speak was Corny who declared, "What are we going to do? It could be that the rest of the ship had become infected and word had never reached the shore of our plight. Or maybe no one wants to rescue us since we're infected. Or maybe they can't find us."

Billie agreed wholeheartedly and added, "We'll be out of food soon other than the fish caught by the boys and the fruit. How are the children going to be able to survive?"

Now was a perfect time for Jacob Cumberland to pontificate on his credentials, "As you all may know, I graduated head of my class at Berkeley, and you may not be aware I received my MBA from Stanford. While at Berkeley, I had the opportunity to take an elective in the causes of downfalls of historical civilizations. My knowledge and proper planning should enable us to survive here as long as necessary," expounded Jacob.

"Jacob, be careful you don't dislocate your shoulder." Billie laughed.

"What do you mean by that, Billie?"

"My point is that you're doing such a stupendous job of patting yourself on your back that you may hurt yourself."

"I'll ignore that comment and move on," suggested Jacob.

"Please allow me to give a little background of how other historical groups succeeded for a while, then collapsed, and why they collapsed. Some like the Mayans and the Vikings had their collapses driven by several causes. One with particular relevance to us dealt with the strange saga of the South Pacific island/nation of Easter Island."

"The Dutch explorer Jacob," (by the way, a great first name) "Roggeveen made the first European discovery of Easter Island which was found by accident in the middle of a huge island-less region of the eastern Pacific Ocean on April 5, 1722. Roggeveen gave what he initially observed as a mostly barren island its name since he spotted it on Easter Day."

"Why on God's green earth do we need a history lesson at this time?" asked Pinhead.

"If you'd clam up" (an interesting term for new islanders) "I'll tell you why, Pinhead. It seems that the prehistoric human habitation of Easter Island began on a similar very remote island although larger than ours, with no means to communicate or trade with the outside world. The island had no known trade with other islands. It lacked dogs, pigs, typical Polynesian crops, and would have no contact with the outside world for nearly a thousand years."

"You mean much like us, maybe?" responded Corny.

"Possibly, but I seriously doubt it will take that long. Easter Island may be the most remote bit of land in the world in which humans have existed. The nearest mainland is Chile, 2,300 miles eastward, and the nearest island westward is Pitcairn Islands, 1,300 miles to the west. For prehistoric natives to have traveled to such a remote island without compasses would have taken close to twenty days even if they knew where they wanted to go.

"How could native explorers have survived a journey of this magnitude in canoes carrying chickens, plants, and seeds for crops and sufficient drinking water? It seems incredible that prehistoric man could have made such a long voyage and discovered an unknown island merely nine miles wide. But they did, and their expansion from island to island in getting to Easter Island is considered to be the most dramatic venture of exploration over water in human prehistory."

"Wasn't there a remote Pitcairn Islands in the book *Mutiny on the Bounty*?" asked Katelyn.

"Very good, Katelyn. Yes, there was, and the book is based upon a true story. The mutineers escaped to Pitcairn where they lived for many years. The island was uninhabited when the mutineers landed for reasons we can discuss later, but now back to Easter Island. Its remoteness makes it a remarkable and unlikely discovery. It was not until years later those large ocean-going ships were built in Europe, yet Easter Island became inhabited with an advanced civilization.

"There's a large inactive volcano on Easter Island with a crater of about six hundred feet in diameter. The island is about sixty-six square miles. Unlike many other advanced civilizations, such as the Egyptian civilization that employed hieroglyphs to record their history or the Mesopotamian civilization which utilized a written language, Easter Island had no similar means to record history. So we have inferred from the ruins and remaining culture, handed down by word of mouth, how they were able to flourish for hundreds of years without any contact with the outside world.

"However, the most amazing fact about this island is the 397 stone carvings which appear to be legless human male torsos. Most of the statues are fifteen to twenty feet tall, and the largest are thirty and seventy feet tall. They each weighed from 10 to 270 tons. There are about three hundred stone platforms on which the statues would be placed approximately nine miles from the quarry. There are nearly nine hundred carvings, some under construction when apparently abandoned. Many experts consider these huge statues, built by an ancient civilization without modern tools or instruments in a remote part of the Pacific Ocean, to be wonders of the world.

"It's believed that the original inhabitants of Easter Island arrived sometime as early as AD 300, though more likely it was somewhat later than that. Where did they come from? How then could this prehistoric population who had no mechanical machines, no cranes, no wheels, and no draft animals have survived and been able to construct these huge heavy statues and transport them to their resting spot, and why would they do so? There were no large timber trees. In fact, it had no trees over ten feet in height nor strong ropes to aid in construction on Easter Island when Roggeveen discovered it in 1722.

"The Norwegian explorer Thor Heyerdahl, in his book *Kon-Tiki*, proposed that the Easter Islanders came over from the eastern Pacific from advanced civilizations in South America. In turn, he postulated that advanced civilizations had migrated in prehistoric transoceanic voyages from ancient Egypt to South America." (There is a remarkable similarity between Egyptian pyramids and the Mayan pyramids of Central America.) "Heyerdahl perceived a direct connection between the stone architecture of South American Incas and the Easter Island statues.

"Another exciting if not out of this world proposition comes from the Swiss writer Erich von Daniken who claimed that the statues of Easter Island were the efforts of intelligent space invaders with extraordinary implements. These extraterrestrial travelers were stranded on Easter until a later rescue, postulated by von Daniken.

"However, the discovery of stone tools littering Easter Island led us to another popular conclusion based upon the known Polynesian inhabitants. The contemporary belief is that the Easter Island settlers came from Polynesia to the west. It's believed now that the Polynesians moved eastward from Asia in their oceangoing canoes which were large enough to hold eighty to a hundred natives. Even though they had no advanced means of navigation, it's thought that they did possess remarkable navigational skills, even using knowledge of shorebirds and the extent to which these birds could venture from shore out to sea. Understand, however, that it would still have taken probably seventeen days or more to travel to Easter Island from the nearest Polynesian island to the west."

"How could these ancient natives in Polynesia have constructed large oceangoing canoes and navigated uncharted seas by simply looking for and following birds? I find this difficult to believe," countered Pinhead.

"Now remember, Pinhead, as man explores, invents, or creates, there are numerous failures along the way which are rarely recorded or make the news, yet do provide instructive insight for subsequent attempts, trial and error. We learn from these errors if possible. We only know of the successful events that reached Easter Island, not the many that may have turned back or been lost," explained Jacob.

"How long is this going to take?" whispered Rufus to Missy.

"Don't interrupt him now, Rufus. He's on a roll."

"Okay, even accepting the difficulty of successfully traveling in some type of oceangoing vessels over one thousand miles following birds and finding this rather small island, and assuming that the crude stone tools were used to construct the statues, how were the extremely heavy statues moved to their resting sites? And why did the natives construct these statues?" I questioned.

"So let's first summarize how we think they carved these huge statues. The size of the statues infers that there was a large population, much larger than today and when Roggeveen arrived on the island. Also, there must have been a forest of large trees to enable such construction although it is a mystery as to why such a forest would have disappeared from the island. There's a stone quarry on the island where there are stone picks, drills, and hammers littering the ground that were used for the statues. There are even statues in the crater that are in varying stages of being carved. It seems like the bodies of the statues were carved in a faceup position looking at the sky. Next, the back of the statue would have been chipped away from the underlying master stone. It's believed that they were then transported on a ladderlike roadway of large trees by being pulled along with ropes by fifty to seventy natives on top of the ladder. Apparently, they didn't use rolling logs to move the statues. It's estimated to have taken about a week to transport each statue.

"Another mystery is that some, if not most, of these statues, as well as the ones that were placed on pedestals, have been deliberately broken or defaced. So not only do we have the quandary of why did they construct these statues, but why were they trashed?

"It turns out based upon oral traditions of present-day islanders and archeologists that prehistoric Easter Island was divided into a dozen territories with each extending from the middle of the island to the coast. Each territory belonged to a clan with its own chief. Each clan would peacefully construct platforms and statues resembling its chiefs and in competition with other clans. These competing clans were also integrated via religion, economics, and politics with one paramount chief. Different territories had different resources, including some remarkably having an abundance of large trees. Because of the island being remote without trade from other islands, this variation in resources required amiable trade among the clans."

"How would these remote islanders have *decided to and be able to* construct these many amazing statues requiring considerable societal resources? Other civilizations don't seem to have done so. Even the pyramids of Egypt and the Mayans although civilizations much more massive in population are not in such large numbers of statues as found on Easter Island," contended Jacob.

"And those civilizations were not existing on a remote island without trade or interaction with the outside world," remarked Rufus.

"Researchers believe there are four major advantages or influencing factors on the remote island that led to this amazing feat. It turns out that there in the crater of this island's volcano, Rano Raraku, is a superior stone for carving. Secondly, those other Pacific islands of antiquity that were able to have trade and commerce with other islands therefore had limited time and need for devoting their resources to public monuments. Easter Island had no such trade and commerce with other island nations to interfere with monument construction. Third, the terrain and, at that time, large timber resources along with natural elements from the volcano Rano Raraku were advantageous. Finally, the island at that time had plentiful food resources required for feeding the many people necessary to conduct these public efforts."

"You mentioned a theory on how these multiple tonnage heavy statues were transported. How were they placed upright after transported to their sites, and why were they found to be defaced and deliberately broken?" wondered Pinhead.

"The prevailing ideas are that the statues, when they arrived at the stone platform after the nine-mile trip, were pulled up a ramp above the platform. Then slowly the upper portion of the statue was raised slightly, a stone placed underneath the slightly raised statue, and then levered again and again until the angle of the statues was such that it could gradually be lowered down into a cavity in the base stone. The actual statue is constructed at an angle as opposed to exactly vertical in order to aid in this final tilting upright of the statue. This method for transporting and uprighting can be deduced also from many other prehistoric civilizations of which we know more such as Egypt's pyramids, Stonehenge, the Incas, and Teotihuacan."

"Where did they get the long ropes necessary to pull the statues and upright them?" questioned Missy.

"The thick long ropes would have been made from a fibrous bark found in South America and Polynesia called *Burweed*."

"But you said that the Spanish explorer Roggeveen did not find strong tall trees on the Easter Island to make the ropes and ladderway for transport and uprighting. What gives?" asked Missy.

"This is possibly the most important insight that the collapse of Easter Island can provide us. There have been recovered remains of vanished plants, palm pollen, and fossilized palm nuts on Easter Island, yet it's from palms not now existing on this barren wasteland of today. These palm nuts turned out to be very similar to those of the world's largest existing palm tree, the Chilean wine palm, which grows up to sixty-five feet tall and three feet in diameter. There are even remains in the lava flows from hundreds of thousands of years ago indicating palm trunks seven feet in diameter.

"Apparently, at one time Easter Island was a tropical forest of tall trees and woody bushes. Easter Islanders could have used these types of palms for housing construction, canoes, ladder transportation of the statues, and rafts.

"Even though there is nothing to indicate that rafts or sailing vessels were ever used by Easter Islanders to reach the outside world, these types of vessels would have been useful for fishing in deep waters outside the island. Excavations on the island of human bones have shown that the inhabitants ate the common dolphinfish, *mahi-mahi*, that can only be caught offshore via oceangoing canoes possibly using harpoons. The Chilean wine palm can also be used for fermenting wine, making honey and sugar. Its fronds are ideal for house thatching, baskets, and boat sails."

"How did they make canoes out of huge trees?" questioned Katelyn.

"Many other islanders, upon which we have history, would take the trunk of a large tree and use fire to break down the wood into the center of the log. Then they'd use stone if available or shell scrapers if not to hollow it out. Easter Islanders had stone available and might have used obsidian stone from the volcano crater to hollow out the middle. Two trunks could have been lashed together to carry as many as forty natives.

"Okay, if perhaps this is how the first inhabitants on Easter Island flourished for hundreds of years, why did they finally fail?" I asked.

"Their collapse is fascinating and needs to be a lesson for us, which is why I wished to share this with everyone. Let's summarize some important factors that are believed to have led to Easter Islands zenith and later disappeared. The huge trees, of which we have historical evidence, could have provided timber and the sources of rope but, unfortunately, are no longer there. At the time of these early immigrants, there were at least six species of land birds on the island including herons, rails, parrots, and even owls. Today they are gone. Easter Island apparently, at that time of discovery, was one of the richest breeding grounds in the entire Pacific for seabirds, including albatross, boobies, frigates, fulmars, petrels, prions, shearwaters, storm petrels, terns, and tropic birds. It is no longer such. There were even seals on the island.

"Excavations of the bones of the first human settlers tell us that their native diets included many of these vanished birds, seals, and as I mentioned before, the common dolphinfish. Their fish intake was relatively modest. There is evidence of sea turtles in their diets and, I hate to say, even rats."

It was now getting late in the day, and Bobby recommended we retire and continue this conversation the next day: day 24.

*****

We reconvened the following morning. "So why the disappearance of large timber and all this food source?" asked Bobby.

"The vanishing of these birds, some now extinct, was due to overhunting by the settlers. There was deforestation, which I'll discuss next, and predation by rats. Even shellfish, mainly cowry and snail shells, diminished in numbers due to overharvesting.

"The deforestation was due to overuse, lack of management and planning, and possibly drought. The Easter Islanders used these huge trees for firewood, cremation of the deceased, seaworthy canoes, shelter, clearing of land for planting, and as I previously mentioned, the transportation of statues.

"This deforestation via excessive harvesting would have occurred during the three-hundred-peak period years, at its high point around AD 1400, of the society [our country, America, may need to be mindful of three-hundred-peak period years for Easter Island, as it has been about 250 years since our country's establishment], resulting in no forest of large trees at the time of the island's discovery by Roggeveen around 1700.

"This bleak outcome of the loss of timber and ropes [overharvesting of the Burweed] ended transport and erection of the largest statues and seagoing canoes. Deforestation also meant the loss of fuel for warmth and cooking, no more cremation of bodies. Most sources of wild food, such as palm nuts and Malay apples, were lost, as erosion of rich fertile soil ensued due to the absence of sheltering trees from rain downpours. Deforestation meant no more seagoing canoes, and therefore, large fish could no longer be harpooned with the absence of replacement seagoing canoes.

"The cruel, horrible consequences for the islanders meant starvation evidenced graphically by the creation of little statues depicting starving humans with protruding bones and hollow cheeks. As in other societies that have had such calamitous collapse, cannibalism began as a source of meat.

"It is believed that by the early 1700s, the population had declined by 70 percent from its peak. As the leadership and promises of their chiefs and priests eroded, civil chaos became rampant, and the formerly complex society collapsed. With an overwhelming sense of tragedy, islanders and rival clans not only took to thievery and lawlessness but to the desecration of their ancestors' monumental work, statues.

"In essence, the downfall of Easter's society was not that they were evil people, or even that they were so isolated. However, they did live in a fragile environment with limited resources and were unwise in their use of it.

"What caused the downfall of the Mayans and Vikings that you mentioned?" questioned Clevis.

"The advanced civilization of the Mayans in Central America and the Vikings colonies in Iceland, Greenland, and Vinland were caused by a multitude of factors that could be a lesson for us: the Mayan population outstripped its resources, ignored environmental impacts especially deforestation and erosion, and its leaders took no remedial action.

"Greenland was colonized for about three hundred to four hundred years by the Norse Vikings of Scandinavia. They also colonized Iceland for nearly a thousand years yet failed in their attempt to colonize Vinland [Newfoundland], deserting it after less than fifty years there. One of the major reasons for their failure to continue their presence in Greenland was similar to Easter Island's deforestation. Their deforestation problems began with their propensity to cut or burn trees and shrubs to clear land.

"Although Greenland is a large island, the fertile forest and grassland's capability is limited to a small portion of the island. The trees and shrubs are more effective at holding soil than grass although grass certainly helps. With the departure of the large trees, grass still would grow without the trees, yet eventually, the immigrant residents' herds of sheep and goats grazing destroyed the grass which regenerates slowly in Greenland's climate. After the grass cover was destroyed, the exposed fertile soil was eroded by the heavy rains. Once the topsoil was removed from the fertile river valleys, sand became exposed and was blown by the winds.

"In essence, the Norse inadvertently made the land useless by burning the trees for heat or cutting down the trees and shrubs for building purposes, boats, etc. We, my fellow islanders, must not be so foolish to ignore these lessons from Easter Island and Greenland."

"Okay, your history session was intriguing, and I understand some of the similarities. But our calamity is different. How directly does the collapse of that ancient society have to do with us? We're gonna be rescued someday, soon I hope, and should make the most out of our current resources and situation," asserted Billie.

"My point in telling you this true story of failure in Greenland is that they *could* have survived even though isolated and alone. However, they made critical mistakes by never making peace with the native Inuit inhabitants, who did survive, and failing to imitate the Inuits' habits. It is also thought that the Vikings failed to give up their Scandinavian habits, like diet and clothing, unlike the Inuits who adapted well to the available food sources, primarily from the sea, and available clothing [Inuits wore seal skin in the dead of winter].

"This is obviously not a problem that we have, but my point here is that we may need to be open to adjusting our traditional life habits to be more compatible with our present environment. Unlike Greenland, however, Iceland did succeed while isolated and on a much smaller island than Greenland, and Iceland has done so for nearly one thousand years. Surely, we can find a way to do so on our remote island until we're eventually rescued. We have to avoid deforestation and abuse of wildlife along with overfishing."

"Please, I'd like to add something to my dad's point about our need for planning," volunteered Missy. "My parents have taken Katelyn and me on a lot of wonderful vacations, some in state and national parks. One that we've visited and enjoyed on several occasions is Yellowstone National Park. While there on one of the trips, I read a most interesting story that may be relevant to our need to conserve and sustain while here on this island. The story speaks to the fragility and interdependence of nature.

"It seems that the folks at Yellowstone decided it might be interesting to return some wolves to their natural habitat at the park since they had been previously displaced by man. So in 1995, they reintroduced fourteen wild wolves into the park. No one expected any miracles although they did anticipate that this might reduce some-what the large deer population. As you might expect, this did happen. There was a significant reduction in the deer population, and the deer avoided the parts of the park where the wolves had been reintroduced.

"Now the story gets more interesting. It seems with the absence of deer, that the forests of aspen and willow trees began to flourish. And now things really began to change. Berries began appearing all over the bushes, and so did bugs. Various bird species returned. And beavers reappeared to these areas of the park. As you know, beavers build dams, and dams provide ponds in the streams. The habitat expanded now with otters, muskrats, and various reptiles. The wolves not only diminished the deer population, but they also killed coyotes. This enabled rabbits and mice to grow. Then came more hawks, weasels, and badgers to these areas of the park. Even bald eagles and ravens reappeared.

"And now for the most amazing part of this story. The reintroduction of the wolves changed the behavior of the rivers. With more balance in the rivers between predators and prey, other species thrived, and vegetation along the rivers flourished, lessening erosion. Riverbanks stabilized, channels in the rivers and streams narrowed, ponds formed, and rivers stayed on a more fixed course.

"So wolves not only transformed the ecosystem of Yellowstone, but it also changed the park's geography. Now I'm not proposing that any one of these extraordinary changes in Yellowstone could be duplicated here on our little island. I'm simply suggesting that any changes we make here on our island could cause significant damage to its ecosystem and should be carefully thought through before pursuing."

"Thank you for that relevant and intriguing story about Yellowstone and the interdependence of all of nature. While here, we, too, must manage our resources carefully and plan for sustainability. We must be cautious of our human environmental impacts, especially our trees, avoid overhunting of birds, and overharvesting of our food sources from the sea. We must be wise, and guidance must be adhered to until an eventual rescue," concluded Jacob.

"And the $64,000 question remaining is, When will this rescue happen?" smirked Pinhead.

"Obviously we are all anxious and nervous to know the answer, Pinhead, yet none of us knows the answer. Based upon the growth rate and necessary expansion of unexplored land and islands on this part of the earth, my educated guess is anywhere from tomorrow to maybe as much as thirty to forty years from now. I say this not to alarm but to merely stress that we now need to organize and plan for the possibility of living several decades on this remote island. The Easter Islanders did so for nearly one thousand years, and surely we can do so for as much as thirty to forty years."

A meek hand rose from Karma to which we would subsequently realize that this fourteen-year-old was extremely bright and well-read. "Yes, it's clear that we don't know when we, or our possible children, will be rescued. It is imperative that we plan our life on this island to be sustainable indefinitely. We can do this, and if you don't mind me taking a little more of your time, I'll tell a story of a similar remote Pacific island history of not-too-different dimensions that was able to do so. This island is about thirteen times the size of our island yet comparable to us for a small previously uninhabited Pacific island while Easter Island, which Mr. Cumberland kindly shared history with us, is about 250 times the size of our island."

"Please proceed," signaled Mr. Cumberland with a slight upbraid.

"Tikopia is a tiny isolated tropical island in the Southwest Pacific Ocean. It is 1.8 square miles in size and supports approximately 1,200 people. It has been inhabited continuously for almost three thousand years with little and at times no contact with the outside world. Also, there is an island almost our exact size eighty-five miles distant from Tikopia called Anuta and is inhabited by 170 people. The nearest islands of modest size like Easter Island are 140 miles away. Tikopia's traditional small canoes found oceangoing voyages very dangerous, which helps explain Tikopia's lack of significant interaction with the outside world."

"So how did they survive, Karma?" Pinhead inquired.

"They practiced sustainability, adherence to proper planning, and population control. Almost the entire island was micromanaged for sustainable food production. This is as opposed to other civilizations that may, for instance, have allowed slash-and-burn in order to clear land to farm. Tikopia, like us, possessed coconuts, breadfruit, mami trees, and sago palms. They used the mami tree for cloth making. Their vegetation was similar to what we've found here with yams, bananas, and taro. Incidentally, their experience indicates that yams and taro can effectively be farmed as crops."

"What was their source of protein?" asked Billie.

"They relied upon similar resources to that found on our island, birds, fish, shellfish. They were very careful to avoid overfishing and hunting. And here's an example of how bright and meticulous they were. They found out that you can ferment breadfruit in pits and produce a starchy edible paste which can be stored for two to three years."

"Why would we need that if we plant crops and use the native fruits here?" wondered Corny.

"That way, when perhaps a cyclone or drought interrupted crop and fruit produce, they would not starve. They also found that when close to starvation, one can sustain life on nuts and other edible plant parts not usually popular for food."

"Should I ask how they practiced population control?" A topic important to Katelyn.

"Excellent question, Katelyn. Some of their methods were similar to ours in concept. They practiced contraception via coitus interruptus, celibacy when society required it, abortion through pressing on the belly, or placing hot stones on the belly when near term. It saddens me to say, and I won't go into detail, that they also practiced infanticide and suicide."

My antenna went up when Pinhead asked, "How did they commit suicide?"

"Hanging was not uncommon, yet the more common was simply swimming out to sea. It's believed that many young men in poor families on what might have become at times a crowded island during famine accepted a virtual suicide, or maybe just reckless behavior, by paddling canoes on an uncharted sea voyage.

"As a consequence, the island has maintained a sustainable level of around 1,200 inhabitants over all these years. I know you can do the math, so I'll confirm that for an island our size and Tikopia's density, that's about ninety-three potential residents here on our island. Now let me stop by stressing that I'm not insinuating that corresponding sustainability of a target of ninety-three for our island, which obviously is over seven times our present population, therefore presents little if any cause for concern for us. [For example, Tikopia's capability to farm may be greater than our capability.] I'm merely saying that we don't need to immediately institute extreme means and controls and will never have to if we are wise in how we consider our unknown future and timeline."

Wow, I thought to myself, *this fourteen-year-old young lady will go far in life whether we get off this island or not.*

Next, apparently Billie, in the past, had researched some of her African American heritage and wished to underscore how we should not take for granted an impending rescue. "I hate to suggest a dark thought, but none of us wish for ourselves nor our children to experience the dire results of Easter Island or the Mayans. If it is generations of us before rescue, and maybe our island is not as fertile as Tikopia for enabling population growth, we do need to be cognizant of what can occur, such as a Malthusian overpopulation." (Thomas Malthus published a famous book in which he argued that human population growth would outstrip the growth of food sources leading to chaos.)

"The population of my ancestors' continent of Africa has been exploding with growth recently in large part due to the introduction of agricultural food sources not native to Africa yet are very conducive to Africa's climate. The additional improved hygiene, preventative medicine, vaccines, and control of malaria have contributed to this remarkable surge in population. There are many separate countries in Africa, some of which have become densely populated to a dangerous degree.

"The two most densely populated around the end of the twentieth century were Rwanda and Burundi. You might have guessed that

Nigeria would be the most densely populated, but the average population density of Rwanda, before what became the genocide of 1994, was triple that of Nigeria and ten times that of neighboring Tanzania. This genocide was the third-largest body count among the world's genocides since 1950, only surpassed by Cambodia and Bangladesh in the seventies."

"I'm somewhat familiar with the Nazi's attempted genocide of the Jews in Germany and elsewhere, but I know little, if anything, about that in Rwanda. Could you share with us how that came about?" asked Karma.

"The common perception is that the genocide in Rwanda was simply tribal warfare between the Hutu and Tutsi tribes. However, there's more to it than simple tribal strife that may provide other lessons for us. The growing population tried to accommodate by clearing forests and draining marshes to gain new farmland, shortening fallow periods, and trying to extract multiple consecutive crops from a field within the same year. The overpopulation growth led to smaller and smaller farms per family. Steep hills were being farmed up to their crests, abandoning lower fields to erode from the rushing rainfall creating rivers burdened with loads of mud. Streams dried.

"The deluge of a younger population found itself unable to sustain themselves as new families. Young people found it difficult to marry, leave home, acquire a farm, and create their own household. Young adults had to remain at home with their parents; death of parents created ill will among the families' young adults who fought over the division of their parent's farmland. It seemed that possibly the only way to obtain sufficient food for one's family was unlawful hunger thieves or extreme savagery. Violence and theft perpetuated, especially by landless hungry young people who couldn't farm nor obtain off-farm income.

"Also, as we've heard, deforestation can create devastating results along with the resulting subsequent soil erosion. There, further complications occurred due to overpopulation along with some global climate change creating droughts and famines in the 1980s. These 'piling-on' effects lead to large numbers of malnourished people, especially the poor in total despair. It was not hard to ignite genocide.

As a result, hundreds of thousands were killed, many being hacked with machetes. We must never let our little society here approach such devastating means. We must plan ahead, control use of our limited land and resources while mindful of our growth."

A hush went over the attendees as these marooned islanders now began to better comprehend their precarious situation. As this sobering thought began to sink in, Clevis suggested "I've got an idea. Let's plant Pinhead's vegetable seeds. They should grow well on the island, and with so much sun and rain, they should be harvestable in several weeks. We can allow some plants to be harvested for food consumption and some to remain in the soil for further seed generation." This was met with agreeable head-nodding except for Jacob. Jacob, being the legal minded lawyer that he was and desiring a leadership position with the group, stated that each family should grow its own produce and barter any excess to their neighbor.

Clevis agreed and added that each family should have its own plot of three acres to plant, which should be sufficient to grow vegetables for each family and additionally one acre as their homesite. True to his Left Coast roots, the environmentalist came out in Jacob, and he posited that the remaining acreage on the island become a wildlife sanctuary (even though there was no wildlife on the small island other than occasional seabirds).

I jumped into the discussion and submitted, "It sounds like, apparently, a major tipping point for Easter was their foolish decision to cut down all the large trees. Even though we don't have need of oceangoing canoes, we do need canoes to fish offshore.

"We have all scoured the horizon for site of other islands to no avail. Have we ever thought that there might be islands close by, yet below the horizon? We can only see about two and a half to three miles to the horizon looking out from the beach. So there could be another island below the horizon, and about five to six miles from us that has nothing rising more than about six feet on that distant island and therefore could not be seen by us. If we can make a modest-sized canoe and for each three miles that we paddle, we could see any possible islands three to six miles further out.

"Like what happened to Easter Island, if we cut down the big timber, we limit the capability to make canoes, we risk erosion, and we'll incur the washing away of rich soil. Deforestation can also lead to loss of shade trees for our crops with a consequential hot sun, evaporation, wind, and direct rain impacts on our crops. And we also need right now to begin limiting the number of birds that we harvest for food such that we don't endanger that food source. Deforestation and overhunting must be avoided for the welfare of humanity on this island. We must plan properly for us, our children, and our children's children."

Clevis quickly warned the group, "The land is rich in years of organic decomposition, but due to the type of plant life on the island that has decomposed, I estimate that a year's worth of planting would require a fallow period of five years for the planted and harvested acreage before it would return to a ready state for replanting. We can use eighteen acres of the land for each family to allow for planting and rotate the three-acre acre sections for fallow requirements. By planting three-acre plots, each individual three-acre plot renewal would occur every sixth year. We'll prevent erosion by terracing the three-acre plots."

Rufus then offered, "I've seen a lot of seabird guano in certain areas of the island. We can mix it into the soil as fertilizer, adding to the quality of the fallow process."

Pinhead asked, "Why does it take five years for gestation, Pa? Back home, we replant every other year."

"You're exactly right. However, unlike our farmland in Alabama, the rich soil here is an accumulation of the island ecology of thousands of years of slower growing, fragile vegetation, periodic storms washing over the island with salt water, and a volcanic eruption with airborne ash spreading over the ground, eventually being covered over. This rich soil of shallow depth makes it easily subject to erosion, which it sounds like happened to the Easter Islands. This is why I believe we need this extended fallow period. We might be able to get by with a shorter fallow period, but I hate to cut it too close. If we err, let's err on the conservative side. If this island were a perfect microcosm PD, we might be able to exist with only every other year for fallow, but a good, safe fallow period for us marooned on this imperfect island is five years. We have to be careful being marooned on this deserted island to not let an assumed perfect fit of shorter fallow be the enemy of the good longer fallow period."

Wow, I thought, *my father is paraphrasing Voltaire.* I told you he was bright.

"Pa, I agree that fallow is usually advisable, but I read of a situation in Montana where fallow had caused a percolation of salt from belowground, thereby creating a saline seep negating the good of fallow," which sounded just like something my geek-headed Pinhead would ask. Clevis countered that he'd heard of this, but that it was probably due to the limited rainfall in Montana, less than thirteen inches per year, and our island should receive a lot more than that.

"What would happen if the five-year fallow period were not followed and each family planted four or five acres annually to get a variety of vegetables?" asked Corny.

"Ma, I advocate that we don't do this and that we follow Pa's fallow recommendation. I feel if we simply plant and harvest *more* on the same four or five acres every year and *not* carefully plan to renew the resource [land] by allowing the soil to lie fallow in terraced plots accompanied by Rufus's idea of mixing seabird guano as fertilizer, it would be analogous to what our American government tried in order to combat the economic downturn caused by the coronavirus by huge spending along with printing of more dollars. Recall this futile effort became a Trojan horse of inflation. Our eventual outcome could be poor, unproductive land to plant for our basic needs. We would end up with demand for food greater than our resources could produce. Recall with the extreme deficit spending, our country ended up with flat domestic output/products but at intolerable higher inflated prices that unfairly and harshly burdened the middle income and lower income Americans.

"Do you remember how during the economic downturn driven by the coronavirus pandemic, the government printed and distributed trillions of dollars to keep the economy going and businesses thriving? Well, this deluge of cheap money did keep some teetering businesses alive, yet it also meant improvements to manufacturing and innovations were not vital at that time for a business to thrive. Productivity suffered unnecessarily. Waste in production and consumption occurred.

"Then real economic growth slowed, and inflation increased due to the abundance of easy paper money coupled with less-efficient production. More dollars were chasing fewer numbers of product. To abandon the idea of proper fallow planning and then planting more acreage would be like excessive government economic stimulation.

"We islanders would temporarily have greater and more varied harvests, yet we'd figuratively, and maybe literally, become bloated and less able to function efficiently to survive our inherent predicament.

"Difficult times requiring sacrifice are part and parcel to our world. Nature culls out the weak and cleanses itself with drought and lightning sourced forest fires which damage some but not all. Afterward, it comes back more fruitful and strong.

"However, do you know what happens when you clear-cut the entire forest? The forest doesn't grow back because the weeds and nonproductive vegetation choke out any possible young seedpods of trees for the future. Rainfall without the buffeting effect of leaves and vegetation along with tree barriers then carries the topsoil away. No, we must only plant what we need and follow the use of fallow," I submitted.

Clevis seemed happy with where the conversation had evolved and added, "With proper fallow practice, the future harvests will continue to suffice for our requirements." This convinced the three families that only planting three acres per family per year would provide more than enough food and therefore enable forty-five acres for fallow in aggregate for the three families, leaving thirty-three acres to Jacob's beloved sanctuary. "We'll have to immediately clear all nine acres, to begin with, in order for the three families to begin farming it, and then an additional nine acres every year for the next five years. But that shouldn't be too difficult."

Jacob called for a vote, but before it could be taken, Karma—who was concerned about the possibility of one day in the future becoming a mother, barring any rescue—spoke up. "What if our number of families increases as we, children, marry before rescue? Will the three acres per family of planting per year then be sufficient?"

To his surprise and delight that his young daughter was so prescient, Bobby suggested a solution in which each new additional family could acquire an additional three acres of land to grow more crops if needed. "These three acres, plus one acre for a domestic homesite, would be accompanied by another fifteen acres from the sanctuary as fallow for any new families," added Bobby, and thereby convinced the GDP membership that he, too, was forward-looking. This concept would be termed "conveyance."

Jacob points out that it is only when additional acreage is confiscated under conveyance can private land ownership be established and the sanctuary diminish.

Corny immediately added, "If two young adults wish to marry and possibly have children, we must allow them to do so and welcome them as a new family to the island with sufficient farmland to survive."

The devout Catholic Bobby then asserted, "And we shall have an official Christian wedding to sanctify the marriage."

Missy spoke up, "What if the couple just wants to live together whether or not they have children? They do this commonly back in America." This idea appeared to delight the three Whitehead boys since they were aware as to how this might happen.

"Also, your point, Bobby, about a Christian wedding, I'm Jewish and may wish a Jewish or even a nonsectarian ceremony," stated Jacob.

Rufus then shocked everyone, especially us Whiteheads, with, "Before we came on this nightmare cruise ship, which I hope one day we can rename *A Time to Forget*, I began studying Islam."

"Rufus, when did you decide to study Islam? We need to talk after this meeting is over," asserted Corny.

Mr. Cumberland next took it as his responsibility to bring some closure to the discussion so the three families could move forward. "Let's not get the horse before the carriage. Whether Protestant, Catholic, Muslim, or Jew, we all worship the same monotheistic God. We'll have a universal ceremony with all welcome. Regarding simply living together, I believe I can safely say that the three sets of parents here are against that and don't believe the concept of doing so back home is good for the country although we're willing to revisit the concept at a later date if the issue arises."

Now, understand that Jacob naturally objected to any diminishing in the size of the sanctuary. However, he didn't imagine there'd be any family expansion before rescue and, if there were, could subsequently establish some type of population control if necessary. Therefore, he gratuitously went along with the conveyance concept and called for the vote.

The conveyance methodology was met with positive hand raising except for me, who was becoming increasingly attracted to Katelyn and wanted to impress her by postulating, "What happens when we run out of land on the remaining thirty-three acres in the sanctuary?"

Jacob quickly addressed this question, opining that it would be years before this would occur, and surely there would be a rescue by then. "And I've heard that the Japanese, for centuries, have employed marsh reclamation, enabling productive expansion, thereby adding additional farmland which we might do with our beaches permitting us to grow more food."

I quickly asked, "Mr. Cumberland, won't your idea of reclaimed land from the beaches have less yields than will the island farmland, especially if we cannot employ fallowing of the reclaimed land?"

"Possibly so, Parry, but we'll still have the present island land with its backup fallow," ventured Jacob.

The membership considered this as a reasonable plan, as no one would want to believe that a rescue wouldn't occur in their lifetime. Plus, a yearly sustainable farming plan, as outlined by Clevis, sounded as the best that could be done under the circumstances. The motion for each recognized family to own three acres to plant per year was agreed.

No party raised the issue that there were more family members for the Whitehead family—five, with four being males—and only four family members in each of the Fernandez and Cumberland families. It was decided that an official contract and document should be written to specify these understandings and incorporate the term "conveyance," which would mean enabling a possible confiscation of *an additional* one-acre new family homestead and three acres per new family for planting accompanied by the usual fifteen acres for fallow from the sanctuary.

Note that the discussion and resolution did not address the possibility that any of these three families could have more children, nor that appetites could increase. And we didn't consider the problem that if the two families' children got married, wouldn't it be problematic as to a decrease in size of the original two involved families? And whether the newly married family, initially without children and possibly indefinitely so, deserved a full three planting acres and fifteen acres to fallow. But that bridge [no pun intended for marooned island dwellers] would be crossed when they got to it. No one is sure whether this conveyance method will ever be necessary before rescue, but as a safeguard, the conveyance method for additional farmland will enable a possible solution should such a need occur.

Contracts were drawn up by the green-minded city-sleeker, Jacob Cumberland, and signed by all families. The three families were so excited with their successful democratic plan that they agreed to meet every month on the tenth day under the auspices of their new governing body called the General Democratic Parliamentary (GDP). Mr. Cumberland was elected to a four-year presidency. (The island dwellers would be able to keep track of calendar days and years via Jacob's watch, a Rolex of course.)

CHAPTER 4

Island Life

A year passes without rescue, and we become more acclimated to our surroundings than we had been. Writing down our activities and agreements are regularly done. We also tossed back into the ocean a number of messages that we placed into any bottles which had washed up onto shore.

We discovered ti shrub with leaves able to serve as clothing since our cruise clothing was beginning to wear. We soon learned to love various forms of fishing even though we had to improvise for gear. Our hooks were made of fish bones from large fish carcasses that had washed up onshore, or we made the hooks from oyster shells. Our lines were initially made of our shoestrings. Then we came across a plant on the island that Mr. Cumberland told us was the hibiscus shrub and that we could strip off its fiber to make a fishing line; it worked!

We learned to make hammocks and sleep in them. By this time, there was a successful and bountiful harvest by farmer Whitehead, much to the dismay of city-sleeker Cumberland who had meager success. Jacob came to the conclusion that he is not made to farm; he is made to manage. Therefore, he devised a scheme to do so. Jacob will loan his three acres of land to Clevis under the condition that for the next crop, Clevis will agree to feed Jacob's entire family. (Some deal for Clevis, huh?) The Whitehead family would now plant six acres per year. Thirty acres will remain for the two families as fallow for sustainability purposes.

Although this means that Clevis must work considerably harder in order to farm six acres, this seems okay to Clevis, as he values the additional land as his responsibility to grow what he thinks best as much more important than the additional effort necessary to feed the Cumberlands. With Clevis doing the planting, the Cumberlands's property will produce a much better harvest than if the Cumberlands were to plant it. Jacob clarifies that his family still owns the three acres even though Clevis is farming their three acres every year for them.

Fishing had become both a necessary source of food and a recreational pastime. Back home in Alabama, we used an old batteau to go fishing in the bay. Pa had also made us a small pirogue that we'd take in the backwaters and catch alligator gar big enough to pull the pirogue. We had a favorite fishing hole called Captain Sam's. It was on the backside of an island between the Gulf and Captain Sam's Creek. Between the creek and the mainland was about two to three miles of marsh with small tributaries feeding into Captain Sam's Creek. These tributaries and marsh were a natural incubator for shrimp. Where there's shrimp, there are fish. The tide would flood into the creek and then into the marshes where the shrimp were hiding and multiplying. The outgoing tide would wash the shrimp out into Captain Sam's Creek where hundreds of spot-tailed bass were waiting for dinner.

After dining the bass would hop a ride on the still outgoing tide in hopes of reaching the ocean. However, we were waiting near the mouth of Captain Sam's Creek with our baited lines to intercept the bass on their exit plan. There we would catch as many bass as we were willing to clean; that's the hard part which is doing the cleaning among a zillion bloodsucking mosquitos and gnats. Those little *no-seem 'em* gnats would bite so hard that we often said if they were the size of mosquitoes, they'd kill you.

Here on the island, we didn't have backwater nor marsh feeders, but we did have shallow pools between the reef and the shore which would replenish daily with the tides. And the best part was, no blood-sucking mosquitoes and gnats.

Since we were on this deserted island and we hadn't hollowed out any of the large tree trunks for canoes, we'd have to improvise fishing from shore. Mr. Fernandez would often accompany us boys, and he was the best fisherman I had ever seen. He'd fish with a Cuban Yoyo. The Yoyo is an ingenious device to supplant the need for a rod and reel. It is simply a circular piece of wood he made from soaking some tree limbs in water, slowly encircling them along with a groove cut in the middle on which he wound the string. He'd unwind a sufficient amount of line from the Yoyo and twirl it over his head like a lasso, eventually flinging it into the water fifty yards offshore. He could place the bait wherever he wished. He taught us how to do this, but we were never as adept as he.

We boys did have a lot of relevant experience from fishing in the shallow bayous back home though. I'd thought about setting up a trotline between the reefs, but Pa had given us an idea for catching shrimp and crabs by taking some palm fronds, stripping the ribbons off the stalks, and weaving the ribbons in and out to create a semblance of a seine net. We then took about an eight-foot width of this netting and placed it at high tide across a narrow crevice between the reefs. We used coconut shells for floating the top half of the net and conch shells to weigh down the opposite side. Then at low tide, using our worn-out blue jeans, we gingerly scooped up the shrimp, small fish, and crabs trapped by the webbing. To our delight and surprise, we also caught some lobster and octopus in the webbing.

Our bounty was quickly placed into a small pond with limited egress to the sea, so our catch would stay alive and fresh until it was needed for food or bait; who needs a refrigerator? Today we'd use our catch as bait for larger fish. The shrimp would be used to catch the occasional grunts. The crabs would be used for grouper bait.

I would like to clarify here that we fished for what we ate. We knew our dependence upon what seafood was within our reach and only harvested what was necessary to sustain us. We were not going to ignore Juliana Berner's recommendation: "When you have a sufficient mess, you should covet not more."

Occasionally, when the tide permitted, we'd walk out to the edge of the reef and look through the water as it grew deeper and deeper until finally what looked like a cliff off the reef falling into an infinite abyss. Sometimes we'd see large sharks swimming in the depths or an occasional huge jewfish that we could never catch with our too weak shoelace lines or our hibiscus lines. The tremendous behemoths weighing hundreds of pounds are members of the grouper family and are called Goliath fish in the Pacific. I used to tease Katelyn's mother, who was Jewish, about the dual names for the same fish since the Jewish King David slew the Philistine Goliath.

One day we caught a large stingray. You have to be very careful with a stingray because of the barb on the end of its tail. It's not only very sharp but has some painful poison on it that has actually been known to kill if it strikes anyone allergic to it in a sensitive part of their body. I had read once how Native Americans living along the Gulf shores would take a stingray's barb and attach it to the end of a six- to eight-foot stick, making a form of a spear. So I tried it and found it effective. We'd spear other stingrays, whose wings taste like scallops, as well as gig flounder along the beach shallows. (Back home, we called harpooning of flounder along the beach "gigging," or to some ole timers, it was called "graining.")

In fact, one morning, while on the edge of the reef drop-off, I had my spear with me attached to a shoe-string line so I wouldn't lose the thrown spear, and I came upon a modest size shark hunting along the surface water. I successfully harpooned the shark which would make for some fine steaks and stew meat, and also found some suckers (pilot fish) attached. Now most fishermen would think of suckers as useful as a steak knife to a vegan, yet I'd read how Native Americans used to take suckers and use them like a form of hook since they attach themselves vigorously to their symbiotic creatures of the sea. So I placed the suckers in our pond, fattened them up, and later fished with our lines attached to the sucker's tail. Well, lo and behold, one of these suckers attached itself to a green turtle, and we now had learned how to acquire turtle meat for dinner. And, oh yes, as compensation and thanks, we allowed the sucker to go free after its assistance.

We constructed floating rafts using tied, cut bamboo trunks. Eventually, we learned to build canoes by cutting a large tree trunk blown down by a typhoon. The twelve-foot length of tree trunk was then burned on the top third of the trunk and hollowed out using seashells. I had read this technique for hollowing out a tree trunk used by an aggressive warlike Native American tribe in the Caribbean called Calusa. They'd then lash together two hollowed-out tree trunks as canoes capable of carrying forty warriors. Some even had sails and ventured from Cuba to perhaps the Yucatan to the west and the Bahamas to the north. It's thought that Ponce de Leon was killed by a Calusa warrior using a dart tipped with manchineel's poison.

Oh yes, we had long since run out of lighter fluid but fortunately found, inside the volcano cavern, flint that could be used to create sparks for igniting a fire. We'd drag our two canoes from the beach into the breakers and paddle out to deep water, where we'd go after large fish. Our fishing lines had limited line test, and so to prevent a strong freshly hooked fish from breaking the line, we'd let the fish pull our canoe until exhausted. Then the fish would surface for a rest, and we'd harpoon it. This may sound much easier than it really was, as we had numerous breakings of lines and hooks, but it worked well enough.

Since fishing is what it's called and not *catching*, one must acknowledge that you won't always enjoy a favorable day. We learned to smoke fish so it would last days before becoming inedible. We'd also take the gutted fish and wrap it in wet leaves and place it in a hole with burning charcoal. We'd cover with a little sand and let it smolder for several hours. And this was as tasty as any restaurant in Mobile! The offal from the fish would be used for crab bait.

One day, Corny came up with another interesting activity that we enjoyed. After evening dinner, we'd all regularly sit around and simply chat. She suggested that each one of us tell what they missed most about home. Corny went on to explain the idea was not to become melancholic and sad, reminiscing on what we missed most, but simply verbalize what may be silently hidden inside us. And so we did.

The next day, Jacob took it upon himself, being our GDP president, to share his longings. "There are two things I miss most. One, playing golf, and two, courtroom battles. As you may know, I'm a practicing [I admit that the terminology *practicing law* has a very different meaning and connotation than *practicing golf,* yet I do enjoy them both.] criminal defense attorney, and I really enjoy defending my clients and usually winning the case. Now I know your immediate reaction is, 'How can you defend a client who's guilty?' However, my approach is to simply defend a client who's not guilty of the crime *to which they are being accused.* For instance, let's say a person is being *accused* of first-degree murder, yet my discussions with him or her are that the murder in question is really one of third-degree, not first-degree.

"You can argue that this is splitting hairs, but it's up to the prosecuting attorney to properly charge the accused, not me. Some attorneys argue that any defendant is due the best defense against the charge even if the criminal charge is correctly made, but I try to avoid these cases.

"Many of my clients are African Americans, and I really get charged up trying my best in a courtroom proceeding to get them off. I'm good at it, really miss doing it, and I fear that in my absence, those who would have otherwise been my clients are now not getting the best defense that they possibly could as if I were there. You may think I'm being cocky and vain thinking this way, but a good defense lawyer should think he is the best at his job, should believe, and appear completely convinced that his client should go free of the charge. You might want to go back and review the attitude of Johnny Cochran in the O. J. Simpson trial to see what I mean. Now a few good lawyers may take a humble, soft-spoken, nonconfrontational approach like, to some degree, say Atticus Finch in *To Kill a Mockingbird*, but not me."

"Oh, there's no doubt that you are cocky and vain, Jacob," asserted Billie.

"Thank you, Billie. I knew I could count on your support." Jacob laughed. "And as you know, Billie, I play golf regularly with the boys at the Presidio Golf Club in San Francisco. I really miss that for my outlet and pressure reducer. So what do you miss, Billie?"

"I miss my kitchen. I really enjoy cooking for my family, especially special dishes. Some of my favorites, as my kids and Jacob know, are crawfish etouffee, pompano Pontchartrain, and flounder stuffed with crabmeat."

Corny interrupted with "*Oh*, those sound delicious. Tell me how to make them."

"My family is from Nawlns, and these are all native dishes. To make this Cajun/Creole dish called crawfish etouffee, you need to first make a roux by melting butter and stirring flour in a large heavy skillet. After it becomes a caramel-colored paste, add celery, pepper, and onions. Then depending upon your own secrets, you may want to add parsley, tomato paste, salt, and pepper, especially cayenne pepper. Then add the already boiled crawfish after you've already taken them out of the shell. Finally, serve the mixture over white rice. Be sure to have plenty of homemade bread to sop up the juices."

Katelyn quickly added, "I love your crawfish etouffee, Mom. That's my favorite! But tell everyone what is meant when you're just eating boiled crawfish by sucking heads and pinching tails."

"What Katelyn's referring to is simply a Louisiana colloquialism describing how locals like to eat boiled crawfish. They simply break the boiled crawfish in half between the tail and the head. Then they suck the juices from inside the head, which you don't have to do if it doesn't sound appealing since it's more spice than anything. The real delight is in pinching the tails by pulling off just the lead carapace shell of the tail, grabbing between your fingers that now-exposed portion of tail meat and using your other hand to pinch the tail while pulling on the exposed meat or, if you're a real Cajun, by pulling the meat out with your front teeth and devouring in one quick motion," explained Billie.

Missy offered up, "My favorite is the flounder stuffed with crabmeat."

"Flounder is common to the Gulf Coast and can be caught by fishing or gigging along the shoreline or beach especially at night with a lantern. You do want to be sure to use blue crabmeat to stuff

41

the insides of the flounder," added Billie. "Be sure to also combine the crabmeat with green pepper, mustard powder, Worcestershire sauce, salt, and white pepper as you like.

"I got a recipe for pompano Pontchartrain from Antoine's in the French Quarter. Pompano is a Gulf fish. It's a fish we serve with skin on. And it's a very delicate fish. Pompano is not inexpensive, but the taste is wonderful. It's often cooked with a crust on it. I sauté crabmeat in white wine and butter with seasonings and green onions and put that over the pompano.

"But enough about food, my second love of home that I miss are the theater plays in San Francisco and especially at the Orpheum Theatre. I know Jacob is going to ask me to state my all-time favorite plays there, and so I'll admit upfront they are *Hamilton*, which of course is about Alexander Hamilton, and the play *Dear Evan Hansen*, which I believe, Jacob, that we saw at The Curran. It's a play about a letter that was never meant to be seen, a lie that was never meant to be told, a life Evan never dreamed he could have. Evan is about to get the one thing he's always wanted, a chance to finally fit in. It is a deeply personal and profoundly contemporary musical, and I believe it won six Tony Awards.

"Now enough about me, I want to hear what Katelyn misses most about home."

"Mom, I must admit your etouffee is definitely one thing I miss most. But the other I'm almost embarrassed to say now that we're all islanders living together is, I miss going to the beauty salon. I miss my pedicure, my manicure, my hair styled and colored the way I like it. And I miss the chatting, I do, with my favorite girlfriends there."

All of a sudden, to Katelyn's surprise, Parry announced, "Katelyn, you don't need to go to a beauty salon, and I can't imagine you ever did. You don't need to change or improve anything."

"Well, thank you, Parry, you make me blush, but that's very nice of you to say."

"How about you, Missy? What do you miss? No pun intended," offered Katelyn.

"I miss my TikTok," blurted out Missy. "Right before we left, I was starting to get a lot of positive responses to my dance and karaoke songs. I also placed them on YouTube, but I think that audience is a little too old for my style."

"Old," asked her mom. "What's the average age of a YouTuber, twenty-five?"

"Oh no, Mom, must be around twenty-one."

"Sorry I asked." Billie laughed sarcastically.

"What about your fast-pitch softball?" questioned her dad.

"Yeah, I miss that too. I had my pitching speed up to sixty-two, which is pretty good for our age group. We were scheduled to play a top team from Broken Arrow, Oklahoma, during our cruise, and the world series this year is in Oregon, which would be fun. However, I'm not sure I want to play in college now."

"Does this have anything to do with boys, Missy?" asked her mom.

"*Mom!* Most fifteen-year-old girls' decisions don't all revolve around boys."

"Like what?" laughed Jacob.

"Let's let Karma talk now," Missy suggested to get herself out of the limelight.

"As you know, our home is in Little Havana. My dad being an avid fisherman and having parents who boated ninety miles from Cuba to the US, taught us kids early in life to love the water, and I do. I learned to snorkel before eight and became certified in scuba by twelve. I miss both of these activities which I enjoyed in the Florida Keys probably three out of every four weekends. You haven't lived until you dive Molasses Reef in John Pennekamp State Park. French Reef is wonderful too. You can snorkel there, yet you'll enjoy a lot more with a scuba tank on your back."

"Tell them about the time you and I were diving off Hens and Chicken Reef and came upon the school of barracuda," chimed in Jesse.

"We were diving in about ninety feet of water, and Jesse and I were surfacing, coming up slowly even though there was little risk of the bends. At about sixty feet, we suddenly looked around us, and for 360 degrees in all directions, there was nothing but three- to four-foot barracuda. We had swam right into the middle of a huge school.

We know that barracuda will not knowingly bother you unless you have a shiny object on your body that might be mistaken for a minnow. Before diving, we'd already removed rings and bracelets, so we had little fear. I've got a beautiful picture of this phenomenon on my wall back home. We also used to go out to Fowey Light and see this ten-foot hammerhead shark that hung around there. That was a thrill, but then he disappeared."

"Jesse, tell them about the time you caught the huge lobster off Elliot Key," Karma begged.

"We were in about forty feet of water off Elliot Key, which is the northernmost key and accessible only by boat. I was diving with some friends in their twenty-seven-foot Cigarette, which tells you they're more concerned with showing off their boat than actually diving. We dove all around the boat about three miles offshore and had caught a few good-sized bugs [lobster].

"My two friends quickly tired out, however, and swam back to the boat. But I never get in enough diving and have always been in good shape, so I continued to dive for more bugs. After quickly filling up my net with legal-size lobster, about a pound to a pound and a half each [legal lobster must have a carapace measuring at least three inches and would be about two to three years old], and nearly running out of air in my tank, I swam back to the boat. While swimming back, I noticed a coral knoll that appeared hollow and heard some clicking. Florida lobster will twitch their antenna together to make a clicking sound. Why? I don't know.

"But now low on air and my lobster net full, I decided I'd memorize my way back from the knoll to the boat, get a full tank, and return to the coral knoll to check it out. When I got on board, there were my two fellow divers [they weren't really friends, and they lived way beyond my pay scale] and said, 'Hey, guys, I may have found a motherload of lobster. Come on back with me?' They said they were too tired, and so I swam back to the knoll by myself.

"When I reached the knoll, I heard the telltale twitching, and as I dove down with my tank close to the knoll, I noticed about twenty crevices with antenna sticking out. You can imagine how excited I was. I decided I'd go down to the bottom of the knoll, which was probably fifteen feet high, and work my way to the top, grabbing lobster as best I could. Lobsters are hard to grab because they'll just back far enough into their crevice that you can't reach them with your gloved hand. [You must have gloves, or else you'll get cut by the lobster's spines. No claws on a Florida lobster, which is actually a large crawfish.] It's against the law to spear them, and that would not be fair anyway. You can net them, but when they're in a crevice, you can't get the net behind them.

"After grabbing a few and missing a few, I saw a large crevice about the size of a small closet and looked inside. There in the back, staring a hole through me, was the biggest lobster I have ever seen. I doubted I could grab him and pull him out, as he was so big, and it looked like the knoll there was hollow such that he'd just back out the other side. So I decided I'd scare this huge lobster so that it'd back out the opposite side, and then I'd swim around to that side and grab him from behind.

"As I worked my way around to the other side of the knoll, the biggest lobster I'd ever seen came backing out. I dropped my lobster bag [he'd never fit in it] and worked my way behind him such that he didn't see me coming. Then I quickly wrapped by arms around him, pulling him away from the coral knoll. He was so big that when he began flapping his tail, I couldn't control where we went. My only choice was to slowly work him to the surface, which I did. When we reached the surface, I lifted him up in the air above me so he could not maneuver in the water. Then began the long swim back to the boat.

"We brought him into the Key Biscayne marina where they pronounced him the biggest lobster they'd ever seen in that marina. He weighed about fifteen pounds. I had him mounted, and we ate the meat in a lobster bisque for six months. [Big lobsters get tough, and soup or stew is the best way to eat them.] I know that sounds like a tall tale, but I've got pictures to prove it."

Karma chimed in, "He's telling the truth." She then translated for Maria, "And, Mom, we did eat on that lobster for a long time, didn't we?"

Maria responded in Spanish and Karma translated, "We did, and it was delicious. Clevis and your dad caught a lot of fish and shellfish, which is indeed something I miss cooking and eating. One of my favorites was hogfish, which taste a little like lobster or Chilean sea bass [Patagonian toothfish]."

"Maria, I don't think I've ever seen or heard of a hogfish." Corny laughed while Karma translated.

"Bobby tells me that they're not abundant, and they don't school. You'll find these hogfish hunting along the reefs in pairs. If you catch or spear one, you may get two, but that's about it. Apparently, they got their name from a long, extended snout and several long spines that reach back from their head toward their tail. Is that about right, Bobby?" Maria asked.

"You nailed it, Maria. They usually run two to five pounds, and as Maria said, they're very tasty. In fact, that's one of the reasons you don't see them in the markets. The captains or knowledgeable fishermen keep hogfish for themselves. When fishing for hogfish, we usually use shrimp or squid for bait."

"Well, what do you miss, Bobby?" Maria wondered.

"Not much. I've got my greatest loves right here. You, Maria, and my two kids. The fishing is great here even though I've had to create my gear, lures, and bait. I've got my best friend and his family here, and I've grown to enjoy my new good friends, the Cumberlands."

"Bobby, are you a politician?" laughed Billie.

"No, but I must mention something that I do miss. It's the way Maria prepared that hogfish we were just talking about. It melts in your mouth. However, the best dish she makes, and the best of anyone, is her paella. You know, Cuba was a Spanish colony, and there's been a lot of Spanish customs passed down besides our native language. Paella is originally from Valencia, Spain, and paella is one of the best-known dishes in Spanish cuisine. Paella combines saffron-flavored rice with a wide array of additional ingredients, such as seafood, vegetables, or meat. Although the original paella was created in Valencia, where it was made with seasonal vegetables, poultry, and rabbit, in modern-day Cuba and Little Havana, the name is used to denote all rice dishes prepared in a *paellera*."

"Okay, Clevis, it's your time," invited Bobby.

Clevis answered with, "I'm like Bobby. There's not much I don't have here that I really miss from back home."

"No, Clevis, you're not getting off that easy. You gotta come up with something," demanded Jacob.

"Well, I do miss our get-togethers at the Alabama Farmers Federation, AFF. You know, farming is a tough life, and that old saying, 'Misery loves company,' may be true to some extent. You feel better as a farmer when you hear that you're not the only one with problems on the farm. You also get some good ideas about planting, and the get-togethers are a good source for finding the right seed to plant that season and good fertilizer vendors."

"Tell the truth now, Clevis. It's that annual convention in fun places that you really enjoy?" hinted Corny.

"Yeah, that's true. It's a great opportunity to socialize with like-minded folks. Speaking of socializing, I miss the monthly men's meeting at church, especially ones where we bring the families and have a barbecue. Everyone has friends at these gatherings that they catch up with. Remember, Parry, that's where you met that nice young lady Rhoda Butler that you dated for a long time?"

"That was a long time ago, and it never amounted to anything," blushed an embarrassed Parry. I tried to deflect this topic by asking if anyone knew the origin of *barbecue*, and since no one offered, I explained that when Europeans first arrived, some Native Americans called Taino were found on several Caribbean islands slow-roasting meat over a fire using a wooden framework. They called the cooking method *barbacoa*, which was adopted by the Spanish and eventually became, in English, barbecue.

"Oh okay, Parry, I get it now," Clevis said, sensing my discomfort with mentioning an old girlfriend. "Y'all gotta admit though that it's not often you get whole pigs pit-cooked overnight like we did at AFF."

"Clevis, I've always meant to ask you what y'all talk about all night while helping cook the pigs," asked Corny.

"Corny, I can't tell y'all everything we talk about, but I can say that there's some mighty good joke tellin'."

"Clevis, tell everyone about Rose and Barb, the two tennis players."

*****

Well, it seems that Rose and Barb had been lifelong friends and tennis partners for many, many years. They were in their nineties, and Barb was on her deathbed with Rose right beside her while holding her hand. "Barb, when you go to heaven, can you send me back word as to whether they play tennis in heaven?" asked Rose.

"Rose, if there's any way to do so, I'll let you know somehow."

Barb passed away a few days later. Then a couple of weeks afterward, Rose went to bed and, while sleeping soundly, suddenly had a voice come to her, *Rose, it's me, Barb, and I'm in heaven now.*

"Oh, that's wonderful, Barb. I'm so glad to hear from you."

"Yes, you remember you'd asked me to let you know if there's tennis in heaven?"

"Yes, I do," replied Rose.

"Well, Rose, I've got some good news and some bad news to tell you."

"Well, what's the good news?"

"Yes, there is tennis in heaven, and we play every day. It seems we're all young now, in great shape, and our games have never been better. The weather is always beautiful here, and everyone is so happy and pleasant."

"That's great, Barb, and it sounds just like we always hoped it would be. But what's the bad news?"

"You're scheduled to play a match this coming Tuesday."

*****

Even Pinhead laughed. Rufus next asked his dad to tell a couple of his favorite Irish jokes. (It seems the Whiteheads had a lot of Irish in them according to Ancestry.com.)

*****

Father Murphy walks into a pub in Donegal, and says to the first man he meets, "Seamus, do you want to go to heaven?"

Seamus responded, "I do, Father."

The priest said, "Then stand over there against the wall." Then the priest asked Conor, "Do you want to go to heaven, Conor?"

"Certainly, Father," was Conor's reply.

"Then stand over there against the wall," said the priest. Then Father Murphy walked up to O'Toole and said, "Do you want to go to heaven?"

O'Toole thought a few seconds and then protested, "No, I don't, Father."

The astonished priest demanded, "You mean to tell me that when you die, you don't want to go to heaven?"

O'Toole declared, "Oh, when I die. Yes, of course. I thought you were gatherin' a group together to go right now."

*****

Everyone laughed out loud, and Rufus requested his favorite about Gallagher and Finney.

*****

It seems Gallagher opened the morning newspaper and was dumbfounded to read in the obituary column that he had died. He quickly phoned his best friend, Finney. "Did you see in the paper that they say I died?" asked Gallagher. "They say I died!"

"Yes, I saw it!" replied Finney. "And where might ye be callin' from?"

*****

"That's enough jokes for now, Clevis. Give me another reason besides jokes why you stay up all night helping cook the barbecue," demanded Corny.

"Have y'all ever noticed how the next morning, when you join us, a lot of the ribs are gone? The reason for that may explain a little why I volunteer to cook. You see, the ribs get done first, and we just pick 'em right off the grill for breakfast. Best ribs you'll ever have! Now, Corny, you'll have to admit you really enjoy those gossipin' opportunities that you ladies do?"

"Understand, Clevis, that the word *gossip* can be beneficial or harmful, and our gossipin' is merely to catch up with the community to ensure folks in need are taken care of. So yes, I miss those get-togethers. You know, that's how we found out about the pending foreclosure on the Tuberville's place, enabling us to all pitch in to keep them afloat until the next crop came in."

"Wasn't that also where you heard that the associate pastor's wife seemed to be awfully friendly with that Bible salesman?"

"Hush up, Clevis, that's wasn't true, at least we don't think so. But what I really have missed are our family holidays for Thanksgiving and Christmas. While we've got our immediate family there along with some wonderful friends, those holiday visits allowed us to see our cousins, aunts, uncles, and some who we're not sure how we're related. I guess they're still having those parties even in our absence."

"Now don't get teary-eyed on us, Corny. We'll get back there someday. Parry, you tell us what you miss."

"I can't say, as I miss fishin' so much because it's great here. Otherwise, that'd be on the list. I guess I do miss fall Saturdays in New Orleans when Tulane has its football games. Nothing quite like walking down Bourbon Street with some fraternity brothers watching visiting fans of Tulane's opponent go stark-raving crazy 'cause what happens in Nawlins stays in Nawlins. And I still enjoy going back to Bayou La Batre for Friday night high school football."

"If I remember correctly, Parry, you were a mighty good running back in high school and just as good a partier afterward," kidded Rufus. "In fact, why don't you tell them about that Friday night party hardy that you couldn't find your front door key?"

"They wouldn't want to hear that old story," I softly countered.

"Oh yes, we would," Katelyn surprised me.

Well, I had to say something now and figured I'd try to skip the most embarrassing parts, but unfortunately, Rufus wouldn't let me.

*****

It seems I came home after a few too many beers and couldn't find my key to the house. I always anticipated something like this, and so I left a bedroom window unlocked in the bedroom that I shared with Rufus. *No problem*, I thought.

I walked as best I could around the side of the house, and seeing the window sill was too high for me to jump up to in my inebriated state, I climbed up onto the fuel oil tank that stored the fuel for our heating stove in the house. Placing my foot onto the nozzle that came out of the bottom of the tank connecting to a hose that ran into the house, I stood up, reaching the unlocked window and gently pushed it up. I then lifted myself up through the window, closed it, and told the awakened Rufus to go back to sleep.

As I sat down on the bed in the darkened room, I felt a liquid running down my leg onto my shoes. Fear ran through me as I imagined I had cut a large blood vessel in my leg. Strangely enough at the time though, I felt no pain anywhere, which of course I figured was due to my excessive state of alcohol. Rufus, hearing me, cut on the room light. I then sobered up quickly seeing a soaked trouser leg with a black liquid. I had always thought my blood was reddish and unaffected by the numerous cans of beer I'd consumed. Rufus reached down and wiped his finger across my trouser leg, smelled it, and exclaimed, "It's oil. How'd you get oil all over your leg?"

Now that I was getting sober, I quickly realized that the oil must have somehow come for our fuel oil tank outside the window. Apparently, it had a leak. I raised the window, and to my dismay, I saw a black stream of oil coming out of the fuel tank now that the nozzle was gone. Evidently, I had broken it off when standing on it. Thinking quickly yet foolishly, I jumped down from the window, collected a bunch of grass, and stuffed it into the hole from the broken nozzle. I continued to stuff until finally the leaking black gold (as the Beverly Hillbillies would say) ceased. I then cleaned myself up and went to bed, thinking I'd address the problem further in the morning.

The next morning, Pa discovered the makeshift leak solution before I awakened. As he roughly woke me up for an explanation, I assumed he might be impressed by my ingenuity in saving the majority of the oil from leaking out. Wrong!

"Parry, do you know what you've done?" yelled Pa.

"I know I broke the nozzle, Pa, but at least I saved the oil from draining out," I offered.

"No, what you've done by stuffing grass into the tank is contaminated the oil and the tank with dirt and grass. Now we're going to have to have the tank pumped and the contaminated oil disposed of! You're gonna have to pay for three hundred gallons of fuel oil, a tank pumping, and nozzle repair young man!"

"Six months of working after school painting neighbors' barns finally paid off my debt. But the worst part was putting up with the howling of my classmates about my fool-hearty venture post-party. That reminds me, Rufus, how did they find out about that?"

*****

After some good-natured laughter, the GDP meeting began to disburse. I noticed, as we walked away, that Jesse went up to Clevis with a question, "Mr. Whitehead, can I ask you a question? You often talk of God, and you're obviously very active in your church. My dad brags all the time about what a good person you are."

"Well, thank you, Jesse, but I'm no better than your dad or Mr. Cumberland."

"Regardless of whether you're right or wrong about that Mr. Whitehead, I'd like to ask you, Is there really a god, and if so, why does he allow bad things to happen to good people like us, lost and apparently abandoned on this remote island?"

"Jesse, that's a question that mankind has asked as long as he's been on this earth. I'm sure you can get a hundred different answers to this question. Since you asked me though, I'll give you my belief. I believe he created us to be with Him in paradise, but He wanted us to be worthy. And the best way He could do this was to allow us to earn our way into heaven as best we could although even that would not be fully enough."

"Mr. Whitehead, I don't mean to sound argumentative, but couldn't He have just placed us in heaven without, as you say, 'Having to go through what sounds like a proving ground here on earth'?"

"Sure, He could have, but how would we have truly felt? You see, He gives us a choice of following His wishes or not. If He simply placed us automatically in heaven, would we feel the same joy and happiness that we do, knowing we had fulfilled our Maker's desires for us even though we didn't have to do so? Jesse, you may be too young to understand this, but we humans, when given something for no reason of our own and by someone else, maybe even by the government, appreciate the gift yet not nearly as much as we appreciate getting it because we *earned* it. That may sound illogical to you, but it's true, and you'll better understand it the older you get. And imagine how much happier our Maker is if we do His wishes when we don't have to do so?"

"Well, couldn't God have given us choices but not the suffering if we did what He asked of us?"

"He could have, but then how would He know if we were worthy to go into this paradise that He'd created for us? Which one of us would possibly have done something against God's wishes if it were clear and obvious that God wanted us to make a certain choice and if we did choose it, there would be no pain and we'd be given infinite life with Him in heaven.

"Jesse, God is always with us and suffers with us. It is humanity that is far from God, and it is we who commit evil acts and harm innocent people. God, who is love, did not save His own Son and allowed Him to suffer on the cross. Resurrection is the answer to all sufferings and is the hope for all humanity."

"Okay, you've got some good answers, Mr. Whitehead, but what about folks that don't go to church, never even near a church like maybe in the remote jungles of Africa, Mongolia, or a deserted island with just their mother and father?"

"That's another tough one, Jesse, which mankind has wrestled with for years, and there are numerous opinions on. But you asked it of me, and I'll give you my belief again. I believe our Good Lord placed a moral compass inside all of us that warns us every time we're getting ready to do something against His wishes. This compass also has the capability to indicate to us afterward if we've accomplished His wish of us. That internal compass in us is our conscious and tells us if we just listen that there is a God. And if someone tells you they don't have a conscious, they've been making the wrong choices for a long time and have chosen to keep ignoring the compass, Jesse.

"Jesse, my belief is that God is love. If you believe in God and are a good person, I believe you have a good chance for heaven. If you don't believe in God yet are a good person, I believe you may just die. And if you do or do not believe in God and are a bad person, you could end up in a very hot place.

"Jesse, I cannot prove mathematically to you that there is a God, and I don't believe anyone can. Nor can anyone disprove it. That's the way He wanted it.

"If you, like many others, are troubled, confused, and don't understand why you should believe in a God who doesn't openly reveal Himself to you, think about a simple rationale which one of the smartest men of the seventeenth century postulated. The famous French mathematician, theologian, physicist, writer, and philosopher, Blaise Pascal, scribbled down on a scratch sheet of paper a simple reason to believe, which came to be called Pascal's Wager. Pascal posits that we humans wager with our lives that God either exists or does not. He argues that a rational person should live as though God does exist and seek to believe in God. If God does not exist, such a person will have only a finite loss (some pleasures, luxury, etc.). Whereas if God does exist, he stands to receive infinite gains (as represented by eternity in heaven) and avoid infinite losses (eternity in hell).

"Now I'll grant you that this logic alone is a naive reason to so believe, will not by itself engender deep-seated devotion and falls far short of what our Good Lord wishes of us. Yet it can at least get us on the path of prayer and pursuit of faith. Pascal insists that men must be brought to God through Jesus Christ alone because a creature could never know the infinite if Jesus had not descended to assume the proportions of man's fallen state."

"Lee Strobel, an atheist and *Chicago Tribune* journalist, wrote a *New York Times* bestseller titled *The Case for Christ* based upon an investigation he undertook to disprove Jesus as the son of God. He examined a dozen experts with doctorates from schools such as Cambridge and Princeton in his effort. However, he failed to so disprove, became a devout Christian, and has written widely on the topic of belief.

"In the end though, Jesse, unless you are so blessed to observe a miracle or revelation, faith that there is a God and He's watching over you is based upon your personal pursuit, your questioning, your prayers, and allowing God to enter your life. Finally, Jesse, if you'll just give this faith in Him half a chance, He'll more than meet you halfway and help you through the rest of the way."

CHAPTER 5

Suicide

Life over these years had gotten routine and, I'd have to say, boring. There's only so much you can do on a deserted island without much reading material (in fact, none that hadn't already been read several times) and not much paper to write upon although we did seem to have plenty of pens and even some pencils. As I was saying, we fished a lot; swam; surfed (one side of the island was not ringed with coral and had a nice beach with good surf); made up games like horseshoes using our own shoes, bocce ball using coconuts, scavenger hunts, checkers on the beach with palm nuts as the checkers, and stickball. And we all told stories, some true and some not-so-true, but no one really cared as long as it was surprising and entertaining. Food choices were limited, and the weather was quite constant; even beautiful can get boring.

One morning, Pinhead and Rufus were out body surfing by themselves on one side of the island. Suddenly Rufus came running up to Pa, Mrs. Cumberland, and me who were all doing some cultivating in one of our crop fields, yelling, "Pinhead is going out into the ocean to kill himself!" We four ran to the beach and saw Pinhead walking through the surf toward the ocean. The two adults began yelling to him as they ran through the water to reach him. By the time they got close, Pinhead was over his head and underwater. Pa was the first to get close and dove down to grab Pinhead by the hair pulling him to the surface. He then encircled his arm around

Pinhead's neck and began swimming back to shallow water. Pinhead seemed to be fighting my father, but my father is a really big man and is quite strong from years as a farmer and gradually brought him in coughing as the two came onshore.

"What the hell were you doing, Pinhead!" gasped my father.

"Trying to drown. We're never going to get rescued from this damn island, and there's no reason for me to be here. You folks don't need me and will be better off without me," cried Pinhead.

Tears cascaded down my father's checks, and he immediately hugged Pinhead, almost squeezing his breath away. "What are you saying? Don't you realize you are as much a part of this family as anyone here, and we could never be the same without you. You're even being selfish to desert us as we do need you. We're all in this together, and we're a family unit. One breakdown and we all suffer. You're a link in this family chain. Son, if you ever did leave us like this, I could never be the same, nor could your mother," proclaimed my dad.

Mrs. Cumberland listened and then softly touched my father's arm and said, "Clevis, you and Rufus go back. Pinhead and I will follow. I want to talk a little with him." Her words sounded so soothing and sincere, plus Pa was so emotionally drained that he and I walked on ahead.

We never found out what Mrs. Cumberland told Pinhead, but he never tried this again. His attitude didn't change much after that although he wasn't quite as melancholic as before. You see, Pinhead had always been a dour, sad kind of person. One of the reasons they were going on this cruise was to cheer him up. Pinhead was never much of an athlete like me. Didn't care much for girls, just enjoyed computer games, which were nonexistent on the island. He was an average student in school, which was ironic because I'd heard mom say that he was the smartest of us three boys and almost genius level with a 139 IQ score. He just never seemed inspired or motivated.

For a couple of weeks after this near tragedy, Mrs. Cumberland seemed to take him under her wing although it didn't seem to sink in much with Pinhead. Finally, one day, Mrs. Cumberland took Mom and Dad aside and exclaimed, "I don't think Pinhead is getting any happier, and I don't think my suggestions are getting through to him. He just doesn't seem to like folks telling him what to do or think."

"You're telling Clevis and me something we've grown to know and live with over the years," sighed Corny. "He's so drat smart that we can't seem to reach him, and it's getting worse. This isolation on the island has made it more difficult for him although I'm not sure it's been harmful for him to be unable to get on his computer pad here. He spent an inordinate amount of time on it back home."

"I've had a lot of training in psychology. In fact, I've got a master's degree from Stanford. I'd like to try a technique to help Pinhead, but it'll require that all five youngsters participate together in a joint discussion session for maybe an hour to two every week for several weeks. Can I try it?"

"We'd be deeply indebted for anything you could try although I doubt it'll work. I know I can get Parry and Rufus to participate. I'll ask Bobby, and I'm sure he'll get Karma and Jesse to join in. Can you get Katelyn and Missy to come? And of course, we'll need Jacob's approval."

"Don't worry, both my girls will be there just to be with your boys. I don't know if you've noticed, but they've become fast friends and it may be becoming personal. And trust me, I can handle Jacob."

And so the sessions began as simply discussion sessions described as a means for young adults to vent with the only adult there, being Mrs. Cumberland acting as our facilitator. Nothing recorded (how could we record), just verbalization of issues and thoughts. All of us, including Mrs. Cumberland, were encouraged to speak, listen, and question.

Mrs. Cumberland began the first session by explaining how we'd proceed in these weekly gatherings and why we were doing this. It was, first off, an opportunity to verbalize our problems. However, it would soon become an awakening and awareness by us through Mrs. Cumberland's guidance of our feelings and emotional fears growing inside of us all as to our futures on or off this small island.

"If we never get off this island, what purpose in life will we have? What is the meaning of our existence here today and tomorrow?" blurted out Pinhead during the first session, much to my surprise and delight.

"That's a pretty heavy question for us to begin with, Pinhead, but a very crucial, important issue for all of us to eventually come to grips with. Before we delve into such a weighted topic though, I'd ask your indulgence for two requests. One is to allow me to call you PD, and second, I want everyone to speak freely and share how they feel about our predicament."

"Thank you, PD, and now as an icebreaker, let's begin with a common concern. Where are we today?"

"We got thrown off a cruise for no reason of our own. Anyone could have caught that virus," argued Rufus.

Missy chimed in, "Yes, and even then, the captain could have quarantined us down in sickbay until we reached Australia. How cruel to abandon us on a deserted island!"

Mrs. Cumberland next asked, "Why do you think he took such a drastic step?"

Now once again, to Mrs. Cumberland's delight, PD volunteered his participation (as I've said before, he's usually a quiet, to-himself guy). "I think he was scared about panic and chaos on board with the other several thousand passengers. Few can suffer so many may not, I guess."

"Regardless," I stated. "We are here, we are existing even though with difficulty, no one has come for us yet, and they may not come for us for a long time if ever."

"That's a bleak summation, Parry, but all very true. It's something we must each understand and accept in order to rationalize our situation. Don't we need to find some sense of meaning and purpose in our situation for today and tomorrow?" asked Mrs. Cumberland.

"Why do we need to find a purpose?" demanded Missy.

Mrs. Cumberland responded, "Indeed, why? Do you all think we need to do so or not?"

Katelyn started with, "What if we don't? What becomes us? I've heard that the mind, its attitude, and outlook can affect the body. When our great-grandfather died, our grandmother died shortly thereafter, and I heard my mother say it was because she just gave up the will to live. Will we survive without a purpose? Will we become cannibals like Easter Island? Would we destroy ourselves or each other? What if, before we surrender to despair, we have children? What will happen to them? Do they deserve parents who leave them to starvation and abandonment?"

I next interjected a thought going back to Mr. Cumberland's saga about collapsed civilizations like Easter Island and their cause of collapse. "Why do we study these past departed civilizations?"

"Why do you think we do, Parry?" asked Mrs. Cumberland.

"I believe we do so we can learn from them how not to necessarily follow in their footsteps, to learn from their mistakes, and even to employ some of the advances they may have implemented. Some have said unless we understand history, we're doomed to repeat it. Maybe our purpose here could be to leave a legacy useful to those who discover our ruins and therefore are able to learn from us. If we do so, just maybe we can, in some small way, inherently make us and these past civilizations from whom we have learned thereby worthwhile instead of worthless and devoid of meaning. To fail to try is a sacrilege to ourselves and those from whom we have learned, as well as a loss to the future well-being of those who could have valued and gained from knowledge of those who departed.

"I read where a philosopher like you, Mrs. Cumberland, said, 'The worse thing is not failure, but failure to try.' Heck, it seems clear to me that an important epiphany from Mr. Cumberland's tale of Easter Island is the ultimate value of nature and trees and how it has a ripple effect besides a direct impact if we lose it."

"I have read," added Rufus, "that the Amazon jungle may be in danger, has few people living in it, has a lot of virgin timber, which could be useful elsewhere, and it contributes a major amount of greenhouse gases to the atmosphere that keeps us warm. It's estimated that without greenhouse gases like the moon is devoid of, instead of the earth having an average temperature of around sixty degrees Fahrenheit, the average temperature would be zero degrees."

Mrs. Cumberland concluded with a simple question, "Even if our families today and possibly tomorrow with generations after us do not survive before an eventual discovery, would we want our being here to simply be considered a tragedy without any merit or meaning for future generations? Can't we make something of value here for future generations who might discover our remnants? Even still, shouldn't we try to do the right thing and not worry so much about the outcome?"

Lo and behold, PD laughed. "You're supposed to be a facilitator, Mrs. Cumberland, but you're starting to sound like a teacher."

"I know, PD, and you're right to call me out. I just can't help myself sometimes."

"Just kidding, Mrs. Cumberland. You're making sense. Life probably is more tolerable and even enjoyable when you feel there is a reason to be even if we're not sure what it is."

"Thank you, PD. Let's all agree that the end of our cruise was surprising and disappointing. Yet can we find anything redeeming in it? Henry David Thoreau looked at blemishes as 'pure and beautiful like the imperfections in glass.' He observed Walden Pond from various vantage points from moonlight to underwater. His idea was, if you can't change the world as you know it, change how you see it even if that means contorting yourself. He said, 'Every storm and every drop in it is a rainbow,'" contended Mrs. Cumberland.

"All well and good insight, but what if you're in a pandemic or suffering loneliness on a deserted island?" asked Missy.

"This does become more difficult, and understand, Missy, that for what we're talking about today, we're not submitting as the absolute truth or wisdom of the ages or that it applies to everyone in every instance. We're simply exploring approaches for living with the goal of making life more rewarding, enjoyable, and meaningful.

"Regarding your observation about living in a pandemic, one possible approach is to view it as an opportunity to see the world and yourself a little bit differently. Let's say you're an extrovert imprisoned to some degree by the pandemic or marooned on an island. Is it possible to find a way to actually enjoy forced solitude? I'm not saying there is a way for everyone, yet is it worth exploring?

"A famous philosopher, Albert Camus, faced significant adversity growing up poor in Algeria during a world war. He wrote a book about Greek mythology known as *The Myth of Sisyphus* involving a sad figure condemned by the gods to push a boulder up a hill only to watch it roll down again and again. Yet Sisyphus continued every day to push the boulder up the hill. And in doing so, he remained happy. There is nobility and pride in work which Camus is trying to tell us. Camus insisted that imprisoned for such a destiny, as befell Sisyphus, 'we [still] must persevere' in some way. Our task is not to always understand the meaning of catastrophes like COVID-19 or being marooned, yet we must strive to persevere as Camus postulated. Consider how Sisyphus remained happy by owning the boulder, throwing himself into the task despite its seeming futility. 'Sisyphus's fate belongs to him,' said Camus. 'His rock is his thing.'"

"I find that foolish," said Missy.

"Missy, it's just a metaphor, a parable," replied PD. "A simple way to put it could be a formula used by Alcoholics Anonymous, 'Change what you can. Accept what you cannot.'

"Jimmy Carter is known for many things, including a famous adage, 'There are many things in life that are not fair.' Well, if it's not and we want to be happy and have a meaningful life, maybe we need to overcome this unfair event like Sisyphus did by looking at the problem differently," proposed Mrs. Cumberland.

"You mean like make lemonade out of lemons?" Jesse laughed.

"Exactly, Jesse. Now let's dig a little into Missy's observation. Here we are, suffering on this deserted island. I, and many other philosophers, opine that we can change our attitude and possibly lessen our suffering.

"But let's also imagine another possibility that we cannot change our suffering or that the suffering is intense like torture. Is such an existence capable of enabling meaning for man or woman? Paradoxically, some say yes.

"Viktor Frankl was born in 1905. His autobiography says as a youngster, he thought about the meaning of life. As a teenager, he was intrigued by psychology and psychoanalysis. He even corresponded with Sigmund Freud and had a manuscript published in the International Journal of Psychoanalysis at age sixteen. Under the influence of Freud's ideas, he became a psychiatrist and founded a private youth counseling program for troubled youths. He worked for the University Clinic in Vienna caring for suicidal patients. His goal was to help his patients find a way to make their lives meaningful even in the face of depression or mental illness. Later he became head of the department of neurology at Rothschild Hospital, the only Jewish hospital in Vienna.

"Then the Nazis rolled into town, and he of course was a Jew. He was passed a US Immigration visa allowing him to immigrate to America yet felt he should stay in Vienna with his aging parents. In September 1942, he and his family were arrested and sent to concentration camps. He spent three years at four different concentration camps: Theresienstadt, Auschwitz-Birkenau, Kaufering, and Turkheim, part of the Dachau complex. Mr. Frankl survived all four concentration camps although his parents did not, nor did his pregnant wife who died of sickness or starvation in the Bergen-Belsen concentration camp. The survival rate in the concentration camps was one in twenty-eight. One-and-half million prisoners died at Auschwitz alone.

"He wrote a famous book in German about how he survived. The name of this book is *Man's Search for Meaning*, and it has sold over fifteen million copies in twenty-four languages. How did this man find meaning in life in a death camp? If he could, could we also find meaning while being marooned on a deserted island? Fyodor Dostoevsky stated in his famous book *The Brothers Karamazov*, 'For the mystery of man's being is not only in living but in what one lives for. Without a firm idea of what he lives for, man will not consent to live and will sooner destroy himself than remain on earth.'

"Before we wrestle with this idea, I need to tell you a little more about Frankl's life in the death camp in order to better understand what Frankl meant in his book about life's meanings.

"There were punishment parades in which prisoners early in the morning marched up and down for hours in the snow with movements directed by physical blows. A boy of twelve was forced to stand at attention for hours in the snow with bare feet because there were no shoes for him in the camp. His toes became frostbitten and the 'doctor' on duty picked off the black gangrenous stumps with tweezers one by one.

"Disgust, horror, pity, and suffering were rampant at the camps such that some became comatose, refusing to move anymore. Once the will to live left, it seldom returned, possibly somewhat like your great-grandmother Katelyn. Some prisoners would steal the comatose prisoner's meal, shoes, or clothes.

"Eventually these atrocities made a prisoner insensitive to daily and hourly abuse, thereby insulating the prisoner with a very necessary protective shell. Torture and sadism of the guards would drive the herd of imprisoned humanity incessantly, backward and forward, with shouts, kicks, and blows. The prisoners' mantra became submerged into the crowd. Do not be conspicuous. At all times to avoid attracting the attention of the SS was the modus operandi of the imprisoned.

"Prisoners transformed into a stage of apathy, achieving a type of emotional death. The majority of prisoners suffered from a kind of inferiority complex. He/she became insensitive to daily and hourly beatings with this protective shell.

"All efforts centered on the one task of preserving one's own life and perhaps that of his fellow. It was important for the prisoner to have faith in the future, or he/she was doomed. In spite of all this horror, some men invented amusing dreams about the future and attempted to develop a sense of humor, seeing things in a humorous light, which Frankl considered some kind of a trick learned while mastering the art of living. However, once the prisoner let himself decline and became subject to mental and physical decay, he might suddenly refuse to get dressed and wash or go out on the parade ground. No entreaties, no blows, no threats had any effect.

"Frankl liked to quote a famous philosopher of the late nineteenth century. Friedrich Wilhelm Nietzsche was a German philosopher, cultural critic, composer, poet, philologist, and political theorist whose work has exerted a profound influence on modern intellectual history. Nietzsche wrote that if you gaze long enough into an abyss, the abyss gazes back at you. The point here is you need to focus, not gaze, on the reason, the meaning, to live.

"In what some believe is the best novel ever written about war, *All Quiet on the Western Front*, Erich Maria Remarque, who was a

German soldier in World War I, tells about this mental paralysis as a type of battlefield fatigue in which the soldier's eyes become 'glowering eyes of a mad dog,' and the soldier suddenly leaves his post and walks across the battlefield, oblivious to flying bullets in his now solitary state of mind focused only upon walking home instead of focusing on the reason (meaning) to live.

"It must also be noted that Frankl made clear 'that even among the guards, there were some who took pity on us.' And he likes to think that they were rewarded sometime somewhere for it. He tells the story, 'When the American troops liberated the prisoners from our camp, three young Hungarian Jews hid the German SS commander of the camp in the Bavarian woods. Then they went to the commandant of the American Forces who was eager to capture this SS commander and said they would tell him where he was, but only under a certain condition. The American commander must promise that absolutely no harm would come to this man. Not only did the American commander keep his promise but, as a matter of fact, the former SS commander of this concentration camp was, in a sense, restored to his command, for he supervised the collection of clothing among the Bavarian villages and the distribution of clothing to all of us who, at that time, still wore the clothes we'd inherited from other inmates of Camp Auschwitz who were not as fortunate as us…' The meaning of life for this commandant was apparently contrary to that of many SS commanders.

"Life doesn't always end up happily for all of us. Some events are beyond our control. In 1889, at age forty-four, Nietzsche suffered a collapse and, afterward, a complete loss of his mental faculties. He lived his remaining years in the care of his mother until her death in 1897 and then with his sister, Elisabeth Förster-Nietzsche. Nietzsche died in 1900. I tell you this sad ending to one of the greatest philosophers of his time to simply note that sad endings can come to great occurrences, and that's the way life is. However, it is up to each of us to decide how we wish to live our days when we are in control.

"Frankl's quote of Nietzsche was, 'He who has a why to live for can bear almost any how.' Frankl describes in his book that prisoners who gave up on life, who had lost all hope for a future, were inevitably the first to die in the death camps. He goes on to say, 'They died less from lack of food or medicine than from lack of hope, lack of something to live for.' By contrast, Frankl kept himself alive and kept hope alive by thinking up thoughts of his wife and dreaming of lecturing after the war about the psychological lessons to be learned from the death camps.

"The experience in Auschwitz reinforced one of his key ideas that life was not primarily a quest for pleasure as Freud had believed, or a quest for power as another philosopher, Alfred Adler, believed but a *quest for meaning.* Unfortunately, Frankl tells us that only a few prisoners of the Nazis were able to do this. Frankl counsels us that forces beyond our control can change or take away everything we possess except one thing, our freedom to choose how we will respond to the situation. We cannot totally control what happens in our lives, yet we can control how we feel and what we do about what happens to us.

"In the camps, there were the most terrible afflictions, torture both mental and physical, and near-starvation. A five-ounce piece of bread was the prison's only food for four days. Yet what allowed some to rise to the challenge of enduring was whether there was a point to their extreme suffering. 'Having a *why* to live for enabled them to bear the *how.*' The *why* was specific to the person. It may have been to see a loved one again, it may have been to tell the world of the Nazi atrocities, it may have been to help others there as long as they could, or it may have been to somehow find a way to fight the oppressors and even overtake them."

"What was Frankl's *why?*" interrupted Rufus.

"The why for his meaning of life was to help others find their meaning of life."

"Frankl did not infer that man is a prisoner to his surroundings [i.e., did the prison camp surroundings force the prisoner to conform his beliefs, hopes, and attitudes to the unique structure of camp life?]. If that theory were true, then man would be no more than a product of many conditional and environmental factors, be they biological, psychological, or sociological, or in our case, geographical.

"Frankl posited, 'Can man not escape from the influences of his surroundings? Does man have no choice of action in the face of such circumstance?' Frankl's experience from concentration camp life shows that man *does* have a choice of action. 'There were enough examples often of heroic nature which proved that apathy could be overcome, irritability suppressed. Man *can* preserve a vestige of spiritual freedom, of independence of mind, even in such terrible conditions of psychic and physical stress.' The sort of person that the prisoner became was the result of an inner decision and not the result of camp influences alone. 'It is this spiritual freedom which cannot be taken away that makes life meaningful and purposeful,' stated Frankl.

"Frankl explained that an active life can give man realized values in creative work, and even a passive life can afford fulfillment for him or her with the enjoyment of beauty, art, or nature. He opined that not only are creativeness and enjoyment meaningful but that there can also be meaning in suffering. 'Once an individual's search for meaning is successful, it not only renders him happy but also gives him the capability to cope with suffering. Suffering is an ineradicable part of life, even as fate and death. Without suffering and death, human life cannot be complete. The way in which a man accepts his fate and all the suffering it entails, the way in which he takes up his cross, gives him ample opportunity even under the most difficult circumstances to add a deeper meaning to his life. He may remain brave, dignified, and unselfish. Or in the bitter fight for self-preservation, he may forget his human dignity and become no more than an animal. In some way, suffering ceases to be suffering at the moment that it finds a meaning, such as the meaning of a sacrifice.' Frankl is careful to be perfectly clear that in no way is suffering *necessary* to find meaning, only that meaning is possible even in spite of suffering. Provided, of course, that the suffering is unavoidable.

"In the concentration camps, some behaved like swine while others behaved like saints. For instance, Saint Maximilian Kolbe was a Polish Catholic priest who volunteered to die in place of a stranger in the German death camp of Auschwitz, and he did so. 'Man has both potentials within himself... After all, man is that being who invented the gas chambers of Auschwitz. However, he is also that being who entered those gas chambers upright with the Lord's Prayer or the *Shema Yisrael* [the most important Jewish prayer] on his lips.'

"In another example of human kindness, Frankl talks of being profoundly moved when, one day, a foreman at the prison secretly gave Frankl a piece of bread which he knew the guard must have saved from his breakfast ration.

"In times of intense stress, Frankl would force his thoughts to turn to another subject from the present. By this method, he succeeded somehow, rising above the situation beyond the sufferings of the moment, almost as if they were already of the past. 'What man actually needs is not a tensionless state but the striving and struggling for a worthwhile goal, a freely chosen task to which he can focus.'

"In spite of all the enforced physical and mental abuse in a concentration camp, it was possible for spiritual life to deepen. Frankl shares that he experienced the truth in a camp, which was that love is the ultimate and the highest goal to which mankind can aspire. His epiphany was *the salvation of man is through love and in love.* He explained, 'I understood how a man who has nothing left in this world still may be blissful, be it only for a brief moment, in the contemplation of beloved. In a position of utter desolation when man cannot express himself in positive action, when his only achievement may consist in enduring his suffering in the right way, there is an honorable way. In such a position, man can, through loving contemplation of the image he carries of his beloved, achieve fulfillment."

"Enough of the concentration camps. What of today? Frankl cautioned mankind in the 1960s, 'the world is in a bad state, but everything will become worse unless each of us does his best.'"

"Well, what can we do to achieve a good meaningful life on this deserted island? What can we do to make our world a better place?" asked Katelyn.

"What elements do make for a meaningful life even on this deserted island, Katelyn?" posited Mrs. Cumberland. "As a possible lesson for us here, Lorraine Besser of Middlebury College and psychologist Shigehiro Oishi of the University of Virginia tell us that an important element of a good life is one that is interesting, varied, and surprising even if some of those surprises aren't necessarily pleasant ones."

Rufus jumped in with, "Wouldn't each one of us one day simply like to look back on our lives and say, 'I believe I did the best I could'?"

"Well said, Rufus," proclaimed Mrs. Cumberland. "I'd like to conclude with never be afraid to dream. Chris Gardner, a salesman who went from homelessness to eventual success as a financial advisor while caring for his child, was the basis of a biographical film titled, *The Pursuit of Happiness.* He explained his rise to a meaningful life was his choice to give himself permission to dream and coupled it with a plan. Chris advised, 'A dream without a plan is worthless.' Our dreams and plans may rise from ashes and suddenly so at any time of our lives. Colonel Harland Sanders didn't franchise his first Kentucky Fried Chicken until he was sixty-two years old.

"We now need to conclude today's session on the meaning of life. I cannot tell you what your meaningful life would be. You must figure this out for yourself. Yet I can assure you that if you do figure it out and pursue it, your life will be immeasurably better and joy-filled no matter what the circumstances befalling you were, regardless of whether your own making or thrust upon you."

The group applauded Mrs. Cumberland, each shook her hand, and slowly walked back to camp—all except for PD who remained. "Mrs. Cumberland, you are a mighty shrewd human being, bright and wise, and I want you to know that you have caused me to think. For this, I thank you."

"And you, my fine friend, are very perceptive, and we need you."

CHAPTER 6

Cyclone

One beautiful day (most of them were), there occurred an event none of us will ever forget with both fear and thankfulness. PD and I went out early in the morning to fish off the reef. As we viewed the sunrise, it seemed an unusual orange tint. We had always heard back home, "Red skies at night, a sailors delight. Red skies in the morning, sailors take warning." As the sun appeared to rise, the sky became a deep, fiery red—something we'd never seen before. We figured this might signal good luck for fishing.

As the morning developed, the red sky probably should have been interpreted as an ill omen. We had merely caught a few skipjacks, and soon the crimson sky had transformed into a foreboding black sky covering the entire horizon and apparently heading quickly toward our island.

Living on the Gulf Coast of Alabama, I had heard tales of hurricanes that had wreaked havoc from Texas to Florida. I had even taken a course in meteorology at Tulane and learned a lot about storms. Hurricane Katrina, which struck the Mississippi and Louisiana coastline as a category 3 hurricane, demolished low-lying areas to the tune of $130 billion of damage. The 1935 hurricane hit the lower Florida Keys with winds of up to two hundred mph, which was one of five hurricanes to have ever known to hit the continental US at a category 5 level. The deadliest recorded hurricane to hit the US was a category 4 when it hit Galveston, Texas, in 1890. It killed between six thousand to twelve thousand people. Hurricane Camille hit the Mississippi Gulf Coast in 1969, yet we don't know the storm's maximum sustained winds since it destroyed all the wind-recording instruments. Hurricane Betsy, which ranged from a category 2 up to 4, yet was six hundred miles wide. (Alabama is roughly two hundred miles wide at its widest.)

As you can tell, I'm somewhat of a hurricane buff. My fifth-grade teacher told me that the name *hurricane* was the Spanish explorers' interpretation of the word for a Yucatan Maya God of Wind and Storms called Huracan. It became used for a natural storm phenomenon in the eastern Atlantic and Gulf.

A hurricane possesses a huge, powerful counterclockwise spin north of the Equator. The spin is the opposite direction (i.e., clockwise) south of the Equator, as we are here in the south Pacific. These storms are called hurricanes in the Atlantic and the eastern Pacific. In the non-eastern Pacific and Indian Ocean, nature's phenomenon is called a cyclone. However, regardless of what you called it, PD and I knew we would be in for a raging, rising sea with torrential rain and winds possibly with the speeds of stock cars at Talladega. Our volcanic island was, at best, ten feet above high tide. We immediately ran home yelling for fear of what was to come. Even through midmorning, the skies were continuing to darken. We knew not how we could survive such an onslaught of nature on so small an island.

The GDP quickly gathered. The adults agreed that we should hunker down at the highest point on the island inside the lean-to we'd constructed in the cavern created by the now-extinct volcano. If the water rose into the cavern, we kids were told to leave and climb as high as we could on the palm trees and hang on. By now, daylight had turned to pitch-black.

First, the sea began rising, and the winds whipped ten to fifteen mph. Everyone wore their life preservers left long ago by our cruise ship. All of us were terrified. Then the full forces of the wind began hitting us like a freight train, including the roar. We laid on top of each other and even tried to dig further into the sand in such a way that if necessary, we could make a quick exit outside the lean-to. The rain came sideways and felt like BBs shot at close range. Wind-blown coconuts sounded like cannonballs as they bounced off the lean-to. Thunder and lightning surrounded us like we were in the midst of a war zone. The rains and winds blew and buffeted the lean-to, but it didn't collapse. The roar was so deafening that we couldn't hear our own cries, yet you could see our faces in fear and deep prayers that we mouthed throughout the fury. The horror seemed to last for days although Jacob later told us the initial horror only lasted an hour or two.

Then as suddenly as it struck, it wearied of us and subsided into an eerie calm which I knew was the eye of the cyclone. This calm seemed to last about twenty minutes, and then the calamity returned in all its might. It seemed as if the storm were telling us, "Ha, I didn't get you the first time through, but I shall now!" We hunkered down even more, not feeling the fear as much as our now-emboldened grit and determination to not let the storm win. Together, we seemed to sense, "We are survivors on this island, and we shall not succumb."

Have you ever heard of the expression something like, "Out of every calamity comes a blessing, a lesson, and a rainbow"? I must admit that during this tumultuous nightmare of the cyclone, something wonderful did happen.

As we all huddled underneath the lean-to, I found myself huddled next to Katelyn Cumberland. I'd never paid much attention to Katelyn other than as a nice friend marooned together on an otherwise deserted island. Here, underneath our only protection from the screeching, hungry wind, I felt Katelyn's entire body huddled against mine. As I felt her warmth and a tingling in my rushing blood, I gazed into her eyes and saw tears of fright running down her checks.

Man has probably had an inbred instinct since the days of dinosaurs or Adam and Eve to protect the female when in harm's way. And I imagine the female has similarly looked toward the man for protection during such times of danger. Whatever, I instinctively placed my arms around Katelyn and kissed her streaking tears. For one brief moment, I saw a flashing smile of comfort cross her face before she returned to view the rampaging wind.

From that moment on, I would become infatuated with Katelyn, and I believe she with me. She had seemed to look upon me at that moment as her protector, and a wonderful ecstasy came over me as I was determined from then on to fulfill this blissful responsibility.

This joy-filled moment between the two of us was suddenly shattered as Rufus was swept from underneath the lean-to. He grabbed ahold of a tree six feet away, holding on for dear life, yet he would only be able to do so for a short time as the fingers of the ferocious wind and rain tried to rip him away. We had placed a rope underneath the lean-to, which I grabbed and tied around myself, handing one end to Pa. "Pa, hold the rope, and when I get to Rufus, pull us both back in."

Before Pa could say anything, I jumped out, staying as low as I could to the sand until I reached Rufus. There, I looped the rope over Rufus and wrapped my arms around him and yelled to him to release the tree. Then our super-human father and PD slowly pulled the two of us back into the shelter of the lean-to.

Grudgingly, after another hour or two, the storm moved away, leaving behind a wrecked island (and home), but thankfully all bodies intact. I do believe that the Good Lord answered our prayers that horrendous day.

Initially, we wondered why the storm surge of this wicked cyclone never reached us even though we were only ten feet above high tide. I suggested that we were fortunate to be on such a small volcanic island, extending only a short distance from land with shallow water and then the sea suddenly plunging into unknown depths. Consequently, the energy waves felt little resistance for such a short beach and deep surrounding depths which would otherwise be required to build into a tall surge before crashing onto the island. This made sense to me, as I had often noticed—while surfing at Cocoa Beach in Florida—relatively small waves on the horizon then build into large waves breaking on the wide yet shallow beach. "Yet who cares the how or the why. We're alive—we won!"

CHAPTER 7

And the Beat Goes On

Time passes over what we had thought and hoped to be only a brief interlude on this tropical island (never have given it a name). I believe Katelyn and I both felt a little embarrassed over what happened in the lean-to that stormy day or simply feared being the first one to mention it again, or the fact that our families were never far away provided little private time for such a personal discussion. Yet our unspoken memory of that joy remained.

During the silent months that followed, either Katelyn filled out in all the right places, or I just became increasingly infatuated with Katelyn to the point of no return. Regardless of what it was, something stirred inside me, and I thought to myself, *Maybe life isn't so bad being stuck out here after all.*

I began sitting next to her at meals. (Our families dined together regularly, as it's a lot easier and much more social to do this on a small, otherwise deserted, island.) I talked a lot to her then, and she didn't seem to mind. In fact, I liked to think she enjoyed it, as we were the oldest kids and were only two years apart. However, it was obviously something more than commonality among peers. We began going on walks along the beach, discussing our lives back home.

One day, I asked Katelyn if she had a beau back home: big mistake. And she said, "Oh yes, in fact, we've been going steady for quite some time. We'd decided to attend UC Berkeley together after high school graduation." This was not what I wanted to hear, and my feelings sank like a Danforth anchor that we used on our fishing boat.

I mumbled, "I guess you're looking forward to getting back and seeing him and going to college together?"

Maybe she saw my crestfallen face or sensed my emotional letdown, and for whatever reason responded, "I was when I started out on the cruise and only came along to help my parents celebrate their twenty-fifth wedding anniversary, but now I'm not so sure about going to Berkeley together."

Oh my goodness. I was so elated that I didn't know what to say, and I'm not sure my heart would let me since it was lodged now in my throat. I didn't have any serious experience with girls, as most of my time was taken up playing high school football and baseball plus helping my dad out on the farm.

To this day, I don't know what gave me the courage to do this, but I leaned over and gently kissed her. I've never taken drugs, and I've kissed my share of girls; yet this felt immediately like maybe heroin must be rushing through my blood. A tingling of joy and pleasure arose throughout my body, and even that bruise on my knee that I'd gotten when I fell fishing on the reef yesterday seemed to say, "I feel good," as James Brown used to sing.

And to my utter delight, she kissed me back. I don't know if you've ever experienced this type of joyous ecstasy, but if not, keep searching for it. Next, we went back to a lot more kissin'. In fact, I thought I could do this forever, yet I think we both began feeling maybe we should store some of this happiness for another time. So we looked at each other and smiled, and our worlds have never been the same since nor would they ever be.

Then Katelyn gazed at me with those beautiful eyes of hers and asked, "Do you think this cruise and ending up on this island was an accident of life, or was it meant to be?" The look in those eyes of hers was sincere, and I knew she really wanted to know what I thought.

So I collected my thoughts and responded, "From what I can tell, some folks think life is predestined and events are not by accident. Others believe it's indeed a game of chance. I do believe some things happen by chance, and other things are meant to be. This here was meant to be." A smile slowly crept across her face, a half smile with her mouth closed and just a slight upturn on the ends, and I knew she was hoping I'd say this. From that point, we became almost always together except when I went fishing with my brothers or helped my dad with the farming on the island.

Now I know you're wanting to know some steamy details about when Miss Katelyn and I got personal. Well, I'm not going to tell you because as my uncle Jed would say, "It ain't none of your business." (At least, I'm not gonna tell you now.)

But I am going to tell you about the first time it got close. We were just neckin', as we say back home, or makin' out, as some say, when I suddenly got carried away and my brain started dropping into my lower anatomy. You remember that tingling I was telling you about? Well, now it was rushin' throughout my body, yelling we need to be *one with this girl.*

Just as I was about to pass the point of no return, Katelyn looked at me with a scared look on her face and said, "I haven't taken birth control pills in a long time." At that moment, I had only one thing on my mind, and it wasn't whether we'd have a child based on this decision. Fortunately, Katelyn was firm yet tender in letting me know that she was a virgin, and I'd be her first—just not today. Well, you'd have thought I was a puppy that had just been spanked by its master with my tail between my legs. So we dragged ourselves back to camp, hoping that something would work out soon.

Several months later, Pa pulled me aside and said, "We need to have a talk." Pa has always been my hero and could probably still whup me. He already told me when I was sixteen about the birds and the bees, so I was afraid I might have done something else wrong.

"So I notice you and Ms. Katelyn are spending a lot of time together. You really like her, don't you?"

"Yes, Pa, I think I'm falling in love with her."

"What about Betsy Jane back home?" he asked.

"Pa, BJ [she never like to be called Betsy Jane] was my date after the football games, the prom, and it made me feel mighty happy when she was named the prom queen. It was fun being together, but I never felt like we were of the same ilk, so to speak. She liked talking, but I never felt like she heard me. She would ask me what profession I wanted to pursue: lawyer, financial consultant, banker? I've always wanted to use my head, cause that's the way you can make some money, yet I also have always liked using my hands. You taught me that although I don't want to be a farmer, it's too much hard work and risky. BJ loved to dance in a way that everyone would be looking at us. I'm a little shy for that. She always wanted to go to fine restaurants. I like barbecue.

"But now, being with Katelyn is a whole lot more comfortable even when I'm just talking to her. Heck, have you noticed how we both clean up after everyone has finished eating? It must blow Ma's mind after all the times she'd have to force me to clean up back home. I could never wash dishes with the girls back home. How do you know when you're in love instead of the thrill of just being with a pretty girl and fooling around, Pa?" [You might wonder how we got dishes on a deserted island; the cruise ship left us some when they abandoned us on the island.]

"Well, son, I'm no expert, and I don't think there's any one absolute method or set of indicators. I do think though that you just nailed one, the thrill of just being with someone regardless of circumstances. That is as long as your mind isn't focused the whole time on this being a means to get you where you want to go with this girl, sort of like President Clinton and triangulating. We both know what's often on a young man's mind."

"Pa, I'm not talking about sex. I'm referring to other stuff."

"Son, in addition to a thrill of just being with someone, I believe a person should enjoy listening to the other, and I do mean *listening*, not daydreaming. Another is to be proud of her. This doesn't mean that everyone must like your girlfriend, or that they're accomplished in something like say the Honor Society. It's just that you're happy and proud to have her with you. At this stage, you don't need to ask yourself, Is she pretty enough? She must be, or you wouldn't be asking this question. And we both know that Katelyn is a beautiful girl inside and out.

"Love certainly doesn't depend upon what religion or politic or where she wants to live. Now I don't think it's an indicator of love nor a deal-breaker, but I do think it's really important that you both feel the same way on having children or not.

"Parry, does she make you smile and laugh a lot? That could be an indicator. Do you respect her? Would you defend her if, for say, your best guy friend were to say something negative yet may be true about her? Do you like her mother? Sometimes girls grow up to be their mother just like boys their father. Understand, son, this is not an indicator. It's just a consideration.

"Something you *do* need to consider is that we've been on this island for quite a few years now. There are six adults and seven youngsters here. Katelyn is the only person that you've been here with who's both near your age and a girl. What would happen if we were rescued tomorrow and went back to the States? Would you then want to venture out and see some other girls?"

"Nope, I know I wouldn't because I truly love her. However, I have wondered if we humans are destined to fall in love with a certain someone or whether it's simply timing and chance. If I had not gone on this cruise or been lost on this island, and therefore never met Katelyn, would I have never married or found the love of my life?"

"Well, what do you think, Parry?"

"Pa, I said I've been given it a lot of thought lately, and my conclusion is that we are able to love as a husband or as a wife more than just one person. I'm not convinced the good Lord plants only two specific people to, one way or the other, meet each other and fall in love on this earth. I know a lot of folks would disagree with me, and I may be wrong. But I've come to believe that the good Lord creates all of us to love others, and as we grow, this love blossoms differently between different folks for whatever reason. There will be others out in this big world that grow in a way attractive to us, and it's up to us to find them and make that connection and hopefully win their agreement. We must do so with the other person's agreement naturally. If we do, we'll be happy for many years because that's the way the Lord planned it. If we don't, we can still be happy but in a different way.

"My point is that you don't have to search the world over to find your true lovemate. It'll probably happen along the way that life happens, and it's up to us to recognize and pursue the dream. We could be rescued tomorrow. Katelyn could go back to Berkeley and me to Tulane, and our paths might never meet again. And unless we made sure we did so cross, we both could marry others and be happy. However, I don't think I could ever be as happy with another as I'm convinced right now as I will be with Katelyn.

"Well, that's it, Pa, and that's how I must move forward. I hope you understand."

"I do understand, Parry, that you're wise beyond your years and wiser than some of us will ever be. Only the future can tell us how happy you and Katelyn may be. Does Katelyn feel the same way, Parry?"

"I know she does, Pa."

"Well, son, finding and marrying the love of your life is 90 percent of the job. Although if I can paraphrase Yogi Berra, the other 90 percent can be hard work. I would like to add just a few more pearls of personal wisdom that this clamshell has accumulated over thirty years of marriage. These don't have anything to do with choosing your love for a lifetime, yet may ease the process afterward."

"Fire away, Pa."

"Number one is that a man is different from a woman, and I'm not talking about plumbing now. Their emotions are different, their decision-making can be different, and they're far better with their intuition than we are. They're much better nurturing than we men are.

"So when you come across these female specialties, stay out of their way unless they ask for your help, and even then, be careful. Bottomline, Parry, men are men and women are women. You're never going to completely understand the ladies, so don't try. Just leave it as one of our good Lord's mysteries of life. Yet this is a good thing, not a bad thing. It enables a man and a woman to live happily together for fifty years or more."

"Pa, I've always been amazed how you and Ma have been so happy together, where many of my friends' parents have not."

"Well, I'm no wealth of knowledge in this area and could never write a book on the topic. Just ask your mother and she'd share a bushel basket of my shortcomings for the opposite sex. However, I have a few arrows in my happiness quiver although I don't shoot them often enough:

1. Be quick to compliment. Always tell your wife, no matter how old, how pretty she looks, and you better mean it or she'll know. Be sure to tell her how good she looks in that new dress she picked out.
2. The food she prepares always tastes great. Or say nothing at all and she'll get the message in a way she can digest it. No pun intended.
3. I try to find a way to surprise your ma every now and then with something she likes to do, such as when I'd get your cousin Emma Noel to babysit you kids so we can go out, just the two of us.
4. Your wife will sometimes be wrong, but she's always right. That's gonna be hard to do sometimes, Parry, but if you can, it'll save you a lot of grief.
5. Be careful because sometimes you'll be asked a question that may be completely innocent on her part even though she already knows the answer she wants, or it may be a subtle trap like, "Honey, does this dress make me look fat?" Don't answer that unless you're a lot more quick-witted than I am.

"Son, if you'll keep these suggestions in mind, I think it'll help."

"Pa, should the man wear the pants in the family?"

"Once again, I can only give you my humble opinion. I think it depends mightily on the two individuals. Some families have it best with the man wearin' the pants, and some families have it best with the lady. Some families will try to make it democratic with a lot of discussions and heeing and hawing. Perhaps some folks can make the democratic way work, but in all the couples I've been around, the headcount is two. And inevitably, there's gonna be some issues that cannot be jointly agreed to or completely compromised such that in the end the vote is still one to one. Someone has got to give in to break the tie, or nothing will get done. And I don't think to filibuster will help, and, by the way, your ma is a lot better at filibuster than I am. My guess is that with most happily married couples these days, it's somewhere in between.

"And that's kinda the way it is with your ma and me. There are some things that she's better deciding than me, like when you kids are sick enough to go to the doctor or not. I always wanted to have six kids, but your mother had the final say-so there. Some things I feel I'm best at. You remember I took you hunting for the first time on your tenth birthday? Well, not only did your mother not want me to take you hunting then, but she didn't even want you to ever shoot a gun. That one ended up in a one-to-one tie. I won out although truth must be known, I think your mother let me cast a deciding vote. Think about what I just said, Parry. Your mother let me have my way. You see, we agreed long ago, without even having to say it or write it down, which decisions are best left in the man's pants and what are best left in the lady's dresses to decide.

"Also, son, there are some responsibilities that a man just has to do. You recall when ole Bella got so old and feeble that she could hardly walk? Well, it was my job to put her down. If you'd have had a sister, it would've been your mom's responsibility to tell her 'bout the birds and the bees.

"In essence, son, I don't think it's best to have one ultimate boss for all family decision-making. But that's just my opinion. You and your wife will have to work this question out on your own.

"An example of something you two will have to decide together is about spanking your kids. If you do decide to do so, make sure your child knows what they did wrong. And I suggest that you spank rarely and compassionately. It should hurt you more than it hurts your child.

"Parry, I've said enough already, but I must share a few more principles I feel strongly about: one is never, ever strike your wife or any woman. Two, know that your children will often see whatever you're doing and copy it later. You're their hero. Three, the two of you should also find a church you're both comfortable with and attend on a regular basis, getting involved where you can. As you know, your mom and I have done that along with you boys, and it has certainly served us all well. Fourth, never go to bed at night after a serious argument. I'll say this again because it's important. Never go to bed at night after a serious argument. It doesn't matter who's right and who's wrong. If you go to bed unhappy with your spouse, you're both wrong. Eat your crow if you have to, swallow your pride, kiss her and apologize regardless. You'll sleep well, live well, and sometimes even get your way some of the time haha."

I later found out that while I was asking Pa about marrying Katelyn, she went to her mother for advice.

"Mother, I know you're aware of Parry and our feelings for each other. He asked me to marry him. I was actually surprised and didn't expect it, or maybe not this soon. I immediately responded with yes. However, now I'm not so sure. You see, I still have feelings for Reggie."

"Katelyn, Katelyn, I'm happy for you, yet I understand questioning yourself. Parry is a fine young man, yet I know how you and Reggie, back home, felt about each other. Honey, if Reggie had been here, what would your feelings for Parry have been?"

"Parry and I may never have gotten this far in love, but if we had, I can't imagine what I would have said to Reggie. Reggie was my first love, and I still love him, yet I love Parry too."

"Katelyn, I have a few questions for you that perhaps may help: Do you really still love Reggie, or is it his memory? If you were to marry Parry and we are rescued and with Reggie waiting for you at the dock, what would you do? What would you do if you were not married, and we are rescued, yet you still felt this way about Parry with Reggie waiting? Does the fact that Parry is the only young man close to your age on this lonely island have anything to do with your love for Parry?"

Katelyn burst into tears and cried out, "I DON'T KNOW, MOTHER, BUT I DO KNOW SOMEONE ELSE IN ADDITION TO ME WILL END UP CRYING TOO NO MATTER WHAT!"

"Katelyn, I love you more than you'll ever know and will do almost anything for you. Nevertheless, you're becoming an adult making a life-altering decision as well as affecting the life of a fine young man and possibly another. I suggest you pray for some guidance although you must make the ultimate decision. Life would be wonderful if decisions like who to marry were without question or doubt, yet sadly, that is not always the case. Do what feels right to you, and don't look back.'

Then Mrs. Cumberland suddenly laughed out loud to break the tension in the air and said, "Katelyn, remember that song your mom and dad liked by Guy Clark called The Cape with lyrics that said:

'life is just a leap of faith, spread your arms
and hold your breath and always trust your cape'."

Katelyn never told me about their heart-to-heart chat until five years later when we had become happily married on the island. I asked Katelyn how she had made up her mind. She said the answer came shortly afterward like an epiphany. She pondered the questions her mother had asked her, especially this one: *What would you say if we were rescued, you were not married, you felt for Parry the way you do now, and Reggie were waiting for you at the dock?*

"Well, what was your epiphany? What would you do?"

"First, I would hug Reggie, and then I'd quietly take him aside and explain how life had changed, and I wasn't the same person he had known, that I was sorry, and I would always hold a special place for him and our memories in my heart, yet I loved another. And then I would go find you, Parry, spread my arms, hold my breath, and jump with my cape into your arms forever!"

CHAPTER 8

Come to Jesus

Shortly after I had the sit-down with my Pa, I understood what I'd been searching in my heart and asked Katelyn to marry me. In one of the most petrifying moments of my life, I heard the word that thrilled me more than anything I'd ever heard before—the word *yes* accompanied by the best kiss I've ever had. We agreed to jointly send out announcements (verbally, of course) at the same time, but only after I'd asked Mr. Cumberland for permission to marry his daughter.

Meanwhile, it turns out that Mr. Cumberland asked my Pa for what would best be described as a personal *mano-mano* come-to-Jesus powwow over their children's apparent *appreciation* of each other. Pa asked me the likely topic to expect sensing what the forthcoming discussion with Mr. Cumberland might entail. I figured that tempers might flare and deep-seated biases surface. So I confirmed his expectation on the topic and asked him to think before speaking and to control his temper no matter what, as I truly wanted to marry Mr. Cumberland's daughter. I went so far as to remind him how he had warned me years ago when I first entered high school as a hothead with a history of far too many schoolyard fights in addition to physical confrontations with opposing players on the football field and baseball diamond.

"Pa, you remember years ago how you sat me down and told me that I must control my temper and instant reactions if I ever wanted to be a well-thought-of, responsible member of humanity and make my family proud?

"Pa, that talk made a big difference at a time I needed it. There's also something I've always recalled, especially at volatile times. You told me the story of your buddy Father Colin McDowell from Fairhope who warned you of the temper I displayed much too often while playing my last baseball season before entering high school. You may not have thought that a Roman Catholic priest's message could make a lasting impression on a Pentecostal Baptist, but it did. Remember he told you the story of a very tempestuous Catholic Friar Paulus who was a member of St. Francis following?"

"Yep, I do recall that story and how an angel appeared to Friar Paulus as the friar walked through the woods boiling with anger over how the town had thrown him out after hearing the message he'd shared from his mentor, St. Francis. But I can't recall what the angel said."

"I think about it, Pa, whenever I need to because you see, my internal genes still easily evoke extreme anger inside me for some reason. The angel warned him with something like, *Friar Paulus, beware your anger, for anger hindereth much the soul, and dost cloudeth the perception of truth.* I don't know if that helped the good friar, but it sure made an impression on me. Pa, you may want to think about it before your powwow with Mr. Cumberland."

The next day, right after breakfast, Pa and Mr. Cumberland walked off together into the woods in the direction of the volcano crater where the eruption had last occurred and hopefully not to presage what was to come.

When they arrived at a safe distance into the woods, Jacob emphatically proclaimed, "Clevis, I'm sure you can tell that your son Parry and my daughter, Katelyn, have been spending a lot of time together. Now I've got nothing against you or your family, but I want you to know right here and now that I don't want this to lead to any serious affair and definitely not a marriage."

"Jacob, isn't this their decision, not ours? Parry is twenty-one, and Katelyn is nineteen. Plus, what in the world do you have against those two wonderful human beings attracted to each other and possibly permanently so?"

"Understand that Billie and I have come to respect and like all of you Whiteheads and could continue to be friends even after we're rescued. There's nothing personal here."

"Does Billie share your thoughts about the relationship of our two children?"

"I haven't asked her yet, but I'm sure that she would."

"Well, what exactly do you see as a problem here? Certainly, it's not that they come from two different races? Does Katelyn have another commitment back home?"

"Clevis, indeed, the different races are an issue, but it's deeper than simply race. Its culture, its heritage, its society. I don't know if you have been told, but my family can be traced back to Africa, and, in fact, my great-great-great-grandfather was royalty in the Kingdom of Kongo from as far back as the 1600s. I don't expect you to know this with your European heritage, but the Kingdom of Kongo was a powerful nation in Central Africa below the equator and eventually became the Belgian Congo and now the Democratic Republic of the Congo.

"It's true that many Africans came to the United States as slaves, and it's also true that some Black Africans were participants in slave trading. Portugal was the only European country to venture into central Africa to raid and capture natives for slave trading. Other European slave traders usually did not participate in these raids of humanity because the life expectancy for Europeans in sub-Saharan Africa was less than one year during the period of such slave trade.

"The Portuguese would sell slaves to other European countries who would then sell many of them to South Atlantic and Caribbean economies which were dependent, at that time, for manual labor in the production of sugar cane, cotton, and other commodities. Slaves from Africa were also sold to Muslim merchants in Northern Africa.

"Most of the capturing of natives and eventual trading was done as one warring nation became victorious over another. Slave trading there goes back to as early as the seventh century, and I'm also sorry to say that some slave trading continues to this day. I tell you this history lesson, Clevis, because you descendants of European countries know little if anything of African history."

"So I appreciate your history lesson, but what is your point?"

"My point, as I said, is that my family's lineage goes back to royalty. We are proud of our ancestry, what's in our genes, and wish that our bloodlines continue to be of African descent and that we maintain our culture, which is quite different from yours of European history. Unfortunately, it is also in some regions of the US, like probably your South, that mixed-race children are looked down upon and denigrated. Even without children, mixed marriages can experience isolation and discrimination. That, my farmer friend, is why it is best that you and I step into this early affair and stop it before it gets out of hand."

"Jacob, I don't know you well enough to understand whether you are royally pompous in your own rite, or you, like some African Americans, may hold anger and enmity for my ancestors who may have enslaved yours. Or are you really thinking that you are proposing this in the kids' best interest? I also doubt very much that you have discussed this with Billie, or that she agrees with you. Finally, this farmer, as you refer to me, is too Christian to hit you in the mouth for what you have said and insinuated.

"Listen to yourself. You sound like a Klansman of another color. How would you feel if the roles were reversed and I were saying this to you? You are of Jewish faith and therefore believe in the same God as we do. Ours is the God of love, and He says we are all made in his image. He's also the God of Islam. If He wanted us to remain forever in our separate tribes, why would He want us to love each other?"

"Clevis, surely you agree with me that mixed-race children have, as you would say, a *difficult road to hoe*? Many of these unfortunates will be subject to racism from both Whites and pure African Americans."

"That's one of the most absurd, anachronistic suggestions I've heard, even from you. That battle was fought half a century ago, and mixed-race children proved it fallacious and so wrong. Capabilities and achievements often exceed those of the so-called pure races. You're beginning to sound like Adolf Hitler and his platitudes of a pure race, or in his case, Aryan. In fact, our country is such a melting pot that I'm not sure if there are any so-called pure races other than maybe yours, Jacob. Every child is a child of God and deserves respect and dignity."

"Clevis, think about your family's history living in Alabama and the conscious and subconscious effects that have been ingrained into your children, including Parry. They probably have grown up having a Black maid. Your family farm 175 years ago probably had your ancestors owning slaves. Some of those ancestors may have even been Klansmen. And I'll bet your children know their family history, and it is embedded in their outlook on society."

"Jacob, you can accuse me of prejudice and call me a cracker if you wish, but don't you dare insult my children, or I may forget my Christian values. My children know of their family background and are aware that their distant relatives who carved out this farm had five slaves.

"It was a different time back then, and there probably were Klansmen in Bayou La Batre which I won't try to defend, and I can't change history, and we shouldn't try to rewrite it unless it is to make it more accurate. We must remember and record it as truthfully as we can regardless of how painful. We hear a lot, in America today, of the sins of our forefathers, Washington, Jefferson, and Madison, having slaves. I'm not about to try to defend their participation in slavery.

"But I'm not going to forget that times were very different from today. Slavery of all races had been around for thousands of years, and 250 years ago slavery was just then beginning to change in Western civilization. However, change is rarely ever accomplished overnight and in its entirety. It's sometimes a process that can take decades. And even then, there are often varying circumstances such that it evolves sort of like a patchwork quilt of geography before it's complete.

"Jacob, you've given me a history lesson on Africa. Now let me give you one on the South, my ancestors, and my family's beliefs and values. As you may know, Jacob, during the seventeenth century, the American colonies operated as an agricultural society, and much of the labor was based upon indentured servitude. Most of this imported labor from Europe was poor, unemployed, and came to America for a new life. These indentured servants received food and shelter, some minor education, and maybe some skill training. In the last quarter of the seventeenth century, the British economy improved, and the migration of indentured servants to America diminished.

"At the same time, slavery had become legally and socially acceptable in the colonies. With the reduction of indentured servants, importing slaves became a commercial necessity and were even more widely accepted. Cash crops of tobacco, rice, cotton, and sugar cane in the South became the economic engine of America's burgeoning nation.

"Then in the late eighteenth century, Eli Whitney invented his cotton gin which enabled the separation of cotton bolls from cotton seeds at ten times the rate of manual labor. Although one might have thought that all this would reduce the demand for slaves who previously provided the labor to separate the cotton, it actually increased the demand. Increased processing capacity accelerated the demand for exported processed cotton to New England and Great Britain. Large cotton plantations blossomed as well as small planters who owned a handful of enslaved people.

"These smaller farmers were self-made and fiercely independent. Smaller farmers without enslaved workers and landless Whites were at the bottom of the rungs of society, made up three-quarters of the White population and many considered the day when they, too, might own slaves and improve their economic circumstances.

"By the start of the nineteenth century, slavery and cotton had become essential to the continued growth of America's economy. Numerous industries beyond the South benefited. Cotton mills in the North and Great Britain prospered, shipping prospered, and banks in New York and London provided lucrative capital to these expanding industries. By the start of the Civil War, the South was producing 75 percent of the world's cotton.

"I'm not trying to whitewash our history of slavery nor defend it. I'm merely trying to share how slavery came about in America. If you wanted to farm at a prosperous level, you needed slaves. I can't change true history, but I can impact some of the future and have tried to do so with my family values. My children are color-blind, and by that, I mean their perception of others. My children also know that their ancestors freed their slaves long before the Civil War and gave four of the slaves property to create their own farms. [The fifth slave, after learning to read and write, by my ancestor's grandmother moved to Chicago. And yes, this is all in our family records.] Two of the families of these original slaves from my ancestors' property still farm what is now their successful farms. And you're right about my children growing up with a Black maid. What you don't know is that this Black maid, Martha, was paid well and turned down other jobs in order to remain with us. Her African American husband was my son Parry's assistant football coach in high school, and their son is Rufus's best friend and teammate. Both hope to play college football together.

"Clevis, you excuse your ancestor's actions by stating times were different back then. How could something as horrible and pervasive as slavery not have been readily apparent to your ancestors as evil as well as the endemic racism that followed after the Civil War? Thomas Jefferson wrote in the Declaration of Independence that all men are created equal, yet you Southerners forced the three-fifths compromise in the thirteenth amendment to the Constitution that slaves would only be counted as three-fifths a person."

"Jacob, I'm not defending slavery, but to be historically correct, it was the Northern states that didn't want slaves to count at all, and it was the Southern states that forced a compromise of three-fifths for purposes of apportionment in congress. Also, I do believe our God-given conscience guides us in the right direction, and this guidance transcends time. As such, our ancestors probably did sense something very wrong with enslaving another human being. Yet there must have been something to cause men to wrongly ignore the guidance of their conscience (remember, human slavery was recorded at least four thousand years ago, and I'm told it is still occurring in some parts of the world) until this internal conflict was too great at a time in which the industrial revolution was transforming the world. I also imagine that there were slave rebellions which expedited freedom for the slaves."

"Regardless, slavery and racism are so clearly and blatantly an abomination against humanity that your defense as *different times* is sorely insulting and nothing more than a red-herring even if there's any logic to it. This is a reason why we look back on what you refer to as 'different times' with such sadness and disgust. I challenge you, Clevis, to give me one atrocity in our present society, other than perhaps the possible continuation of racism, that our future offspring may look back upon us with similar utter repugnance and loathing as today we do of pre–Civil War slavery in the South."

"Abortion," answered Clevis.

CHAPTER 9

Discussion Continues

Unfortunately, Jacob and Clevis were not convinced yet of each other's convictions; however, they were now more understanding of the other. They decided to reconvene the next day.

"Jacob, one day when Rufus was about ten years old, he came to me, and I could tell something was troubling him deeply. He asked me, 'Pa, why does God make us all different? I'll never be as smart as PD, and I'll never be as athletic as Parry. And there are folks in my class much better at schoolin' than me. I'm afraid I'll never make you proud of me. Why didn't God give me something special?'

"My answer was, 'Rufus, you are special. We're all special in our own way. God did allow some to have more challenges than others and some to have more or less talent, abilities, and skills than another, and I don't know why. Nevertheless, I don't worry about it. We can't all be president of the United States yet never be afraid to be what God meant for us to be. And remember, if you do want to be heard in this world, you've *got to make some noise*! Regardless, we should all strive to pursue our God's wishes and the greater good for mankind. Think about if God did give us all equal skills and talents. Then only one of us would have been necessary, or just imagine what competition would be like if everyone had equal talents. When you and I get to the pearly gates, I don't think God is going to ask you, 'Why didn't you write music like Mozart or play football as well as Brady or even match some of the things that your brothers did?' No, he's going to simply say, 'How did you do with the blessings and gifts that I gave you?' Did you use them as best you could? Did you use them to help others? Did you help guide your children toward Me? Did you stand up for what you believe in? Did you listen to Me when I came to you? Did you treat all my children, your brothers and sisters, equally and fairly? If you did as best you could, because that's why I put you down on the earth, COME ON IN!'"

"Jacob, I do believe this is what our good Lord expects of us, to treat all his children equally and fairly. Our good Lord didn't favor one race over the other. He never said races are different and should be kept segregated. The part you and I are wrestling with today is that perception and maybe even fact that we each are different in some ways. However, our Savior will not ask us of our differences. His only question will be whether we treated all equally and fairly no matter our differences.

"And so, my fellow descendant of Abraham, I shall not interfere nor discourage Parry and Katelyn in any way simply because they come from two different races. There is nothing wrong with offering your advice and counsel. Before you *interfere* in any way though, I suggest you discuss it further with Billie. And after discussing with Billie, my strong opinion will still be that you *not* interfere nor discourage them, as you will risk losing the respect and admiration of two fine young adults, and you and I shall have another come-to-Jesus *meeting*."

The discussion ended without any physical blows. My pa explained to me what had occurred and left it up to me as to how to proceed. Apparently, Mr. Cumberland left angry and very troubled.

I didn't share the events of their confrontation with Katelyn, and I decided to proceed anyway to ask Mr. Cumberland for his daughter's hand in marriage. I must admit though that I was scared to do so. Katelyn loved the fact that I'd thought of asking her father for permission, yet she worried how her African American father would react to her daughter marrying into the White race whether or not we ever returned to the states. Naturally, I asked myself, if Mr. Cumberland were to say, "Hell no," what would we do? How could we run away? There's no place for two in love to run away on a small deserted island.

And so, I did ask for Mr. Cumberland to walk with me along the shore for a man-to-man talk. "Mr. Cumberland, you may know already, but if not, I love your daughter with all my heart and she loves me. We both have thought our situation over thoroughly and discussed all the cons as to why we should not marry. We understand the complications of interracial marriages. We know the argument that we have no other peers here to compare ourselves to. We know when and if we get rescued, that we will then be made aware of others, their qualities, their looks, yet we are absolutely sure that we will never question our decision to marry.

"We have our memories of affairs back home and know they never had the magic and pure excitement and love we feel every day we are together. We know there will be challenges when we return home for a mixed marriage with so-called mixed children, and we are ready to stand tall for our decision. And who knows, we may be a shining example that some others may decide to follow, thereby confirming the gift that our Lord has presented us within our love for each other regardless of prejudices and obstacles.

"Mr. Cumberland, you may be thinking, *Why don't they just wait until after we're rescued to ensure they are right about this choice of theirs?* Mr. Cumberland, we can't wait. We would be living a charade if we did. We are both young adults and are ready to take on the responsibilities of young married adults. And yes, we do wish to have children shortly after marrying. I shall be proud to have your daughter as my wife, mother of our children, companion, and best friend forever.

"Mr. Cumberland I would be honored to be married to your daughter and be a member of your family. I've had this discussion with my father, and I know you and he have had your serious disagreements. Yet he has promised me that he and my mother would love very much to have Katelyn as their daughter-in-law and join their family.

"Do we have your blessings to join together as one, and can you consider me as a member of your family?"

A long moment of silence ensued. My previous butterflies had long since disappeared, and I felt comfortable and that of a man for what I had asked of Mr. Cumberland. I was ready to respond to whatever his answer might be.

Finally, he replied, "Parry, you're right that your father and I had a heated argument on the future of you two kids. I want you to know that I was adamant against you two marrying, and your father was convinced that you two could handle any complications as husband and wife. I admired your father for what he had to say and how he did so. I have always been impressed by you, Parry, and had you been an African American, it would have been much easier for me. But you're not. Katelyn is, and I don't think you, Parry, have any concept of the challenges you and your children would face."

And then to my utter amazement, he blurted out, "Are you going to continue to be a farmer?"

To my own surprise, I quickly answered, "I would be proud to be a farmer, and as long as we're on this island and you wish to eat, yes, I shall be a farmer."

He thought a minute and suddenly laughed and said, "Welcome to the family."

CHAPTER 10

Civilized Island Life Matures
and Becomes Frayed

With the joyous responses from our families, we immediately began with our happy mothers planning the events of when and what would take place. Clevis made a Christian cross to hang before the ceremony. Jacob did similarly with a Star of David. Jacob also constructed a chuppah, which is the wedding canopy under which the ceremony takes place. As you can envision, the wedding occurred on the beach. Mr. Cumberland performed the ceremony, and there were more participants in the wedding festivity than guests. In fact, the only real guests were the Fernandez family, and they cheered and clapped enough for a normal wedding event back home. Afterward, as Katelyn and I walked down the aisle, man and wife, I noticed PD, my best man, with tears rolling down his checks. PD then turned and walked away from the wedding party (and I do mean "party" in terms of a major celebration). I assumed he was searching for some quiet contemplation, possibly pondering whether he might ever be so fortunate in marriage. We honeymooned on a secluded section of the island and began working on an addition to our family.

The next day, a vote was taken by the GDP and approved to provision for one acre for homestead, convert three acres from the sanctuary into farmland, and set fifteen acres aside from the sanctuary for fallow via the agreed conveyance amendment all to be owned by Parry and Katelyn. The already-weary Clevis agreed to farm the additional three acres with me, now becoming nine acres for Clevis to farm annually, "but only if PD will help." Even though PD is not nearly as experienced a farmer as our father, these two with my help should be able to farm the nine acres.

About a month later, PD and I were fishing one evening. The fish hadn't started biting yet, and I felt it was the right time to ask PD, "What was the cause of your tears at the recent wedding? I thought ladies were supposed to cry at weddings, not the men?"

PD looked me straight in the eye and declared, "Parry, you two were so in love in that peaceful ecstatic moment that something shook me to my core. I felt like the good Lord were smiling right there next to me. I was overwhelmed with joy inside of me. For the first time in a long time, I sensed that I was where God wanted me to be—best man at my brother's wedding. I was serving my purpose and experienced pure peace. Parry, is it possible that God graces us in a way like this even though some would consider it *bizarre* or even *weird*? Regardless, I was speechless like never before, and all I could do was cry. Afterward, I scooted over to the other side of the island, looked at a beautiful sunset, and said a prayer of thanks as best I could. You know, Parry, I've never been very religious. Still this experience at your wedding awakened something inside me, and I haven't been the same since!"

*****

Five more years subsequently passed, and some of the children have grown to be young adults. Indeed, it's been quite a few years since the declaration of conveyance had been signed (we started referring to time as pre-conveyance and post-conveyance). After Katelyn and I had tied the knot (you can't buy a ring on this island), honeymooned at the beachside resort (where else could we?), and had conceived a pair of twins: a boy named Clovis and a girl named Venus.

Clovis was named after the original settlers of North America, and Venus after the Roman goddess of beauty and other things. Ma and Pa helped birth the babies without too much difficulty, thank the good Lord. They had birthed many calves and even a colt on the farm.

The growing community is becoming ever more vegetarian with the growth in vegetable acreage even though there is a slight decline in the harvest per acre since Clevis is having to work harder, and PD, although he is very good at farming, is still learning from Pa. There is also a drop in the fruit harvests along with a decrease in caught fish due to overfishing that had occurred in the shallow inlets created by the coral reef which nearly encircled the island. And yes, the population was growing, as evidenced by a need for more seats at the General Democratic Parliamentary.

I must remark here how quickly PD is adapting to farming and really seems to enjoy it. I asked PD one day how he could enjoy farming so much after spending all his previous spare time before the cruise "playing" on the internet (PD never admitted this, but I think he occasionally hacked into protected sites just to show the owners that a hacker could get in). PD's unexpected answer was very profound, "I used to enjoy the how in life, and now farming offers me the beautiful *wow* in life."

PD had also discovered that he could smoke a weed which some- how he found on the island, thereby enabling a pleasurable evening habit. He even sold some to Mr. Cumberland (IOU was employed). In spite of PD's newfound evening habit, he did occasionally come up with a good question or idea. One day at the monthly GDP mem- ber meeting, he asked Mr. Cumberland (who was the incumbent president of the group), "We've only got fourteen acres left unused and unassigned in the sanctuary. At the recent growth rate in GDP that we've experienced and without rescue, sometime soon we'll need the remaining acres that are in the sanctuary. Any population growth after that and we'll find ourselves with more mouths to feed than the island can provide. After all, either Rufus or I will probably want to tie the knot one day with some lucky lady. What will happen then?"

Although this had always been in the very back of our minds, this startling spoken revelation immediately cast fear into many of the island dwellers. Once again though, Mr. Cumberland simply offered, "Surely sometime within the next several years we'll be rescued."

"Well, we haven't yet, and it's been a long time," responded Rufus.

"Yes, but the chances of getting rescued in the next couple of years are greater for each year that we haven't been rescued, especially since we've already been here over five years," opined President Cumberland. "For instance, let's say that the chance of rescue for each individual year has always been 30 percent that it'll happen that year [and we know that it's actually greater than this, but we're assuming worst case]. And in the first five years, for some reason, there's been no rescue. Then the likelihood that there is a rescue in the next year is 100 percent minus 70 percent times itself five times, which is a very high resultant likelihood of rescue of over 80 percent and almost 90 percent for the following year."

This, of course, was not mathematically correct, but those of us who knew this saw no need in arguing or embarrassing the nonstatistically trained Mr. Cumberland. "Yes, that must be right," agreed most of the membership while assuming that they could just *kick the can (i.e., the issue of "when") down the road*. This so-called proof gives PD a headache, and so he leaves the meeting to smoke some weed on the beach.

Suddenly, to everyone's surprise, Rufus barks, "I hear your likelihoods, Mr. Cumberland, although I'm not sure about your math. Even so, what if it turns out you're wrong and we don't get rescued in the next couple of years? We can't continue to borrow land from the sanctuary. Maybe we should start now to limit population growth or how much we eat so eventually real requirements to feed don't exceed real capability to harvest. We don't want to create a deficiency year after year between the amount of food we can harvest and our food requirements, do we? It may be reasonable to eat into our stored-up breadfruit paste in occasional scarce years, but not on a regular basis. Our inventory of breadfruit paste has been steadily decreasing."

I felt like I had to add another similarity between our limited resources (arguably land on the island and beachfront land recovery) and the choice that America had made after the coronavirus to address its economy plight. "I believe Rufus has a good point. Remember the price our country had to pay and is continuing to pay for its decision to insert more money into the economy by simply increasing its debt and additionally merely printing more greenbacks. Inflation was still out of control when we left. Can't we learn from that huge mistake and not repeat turning a blind eye to how we'll ever satisfy tomorrow the debts we're generating today by degrading and depleting our land? All our government did was issue a seventh credit card to pay off its six credit cards which, if it continues, will eventually cause a collapse of America's way of life. Our country's deficit caused by the impact of overspending its resources (tax revenue) is metaphorically our deficit impact by overconsuming today to the detriment of tomorrow's food resources, regardless of whether we're referring to stored breadfruit paste or depletion of soil vitality and fertility. Our price to pay here could be a collapse too on the scale and suffering of Easter Island."

"Rufus, you and Parry are fearing that one day our needs will outgrow our resources. We haven't yet tapped into what our capabilities here are. Additionally, who knows, maybe the ocean will recede and we'll end up with even more land? Anyway, surely someone will come to our rescue before then."

"Who?" asks Rufus.

CHAPTER 11

Where Did He Go?

Everyone on the island seemed to be genuinely happy with what had happened with Katelyn and me. It was as if we all had all begun smoking PD's weed. But like all joyous events, life moved on, no rescue occurred, and we sadly became faced with a tragedy.

My father's family had a history of heart problems, and the men often didn't live more than mid-'60s. My father was no exception and, before he was sixty, had to have two stents inserted into his heart and one by-pass. The fact that he habitually worked so hard from sunup to sundown didn't help. So I was always worried about him, as was my mother, yet he would simply change any subject of his health and say he felt great and it was in the good Lord's hands anyway. I did notice lately that he seemed to be short of breath and with less than his normal robust energy.

It's difficult for most children to approach their father—or at least mine, asking about his health and fitness. I didn't want to alarm my mother, and so I decided to discuss it with Pa's best friend, Bobby. Bobby's response was not reassuring. "Parry, as you know, your father and I have been best of friends since our days in Vietnam. I've been concerned about his health for the last several months, and I told him so. It really surprised me when your dad, who never liked to talk of himself or any weakness, offered that indeed he'd had some chest pains and told me of his family's history of heart problems.

"He made me promise not to mention it to anyone else. I told him I would try not to alarm his family unless absolutely necessary. Parry, I love your dad like a brother and more than any man on this earth, and I feel it is now necessary to caution you about your dad's condition. I believe, at the very least, he should back down on his farming activities, and you boys and maybe Jacob and I take bigger roles in the farming effort."

This confirmed my worst fears, and I continued to worry about my father's condition and his health. You have to understand that Pa was not only my father, but my best friend, and of my utmost respect and admiration. Several weeks later of anxiety over my father's health accompanied by considerable prayers, I decided to discuss this with our family the next day.

However, before I could do so that next morning when we arose for breakfast, Pa wasn't there although this wasn't completely unusual, as he often went out to the fields early before anyone else arose. But even whenever he'd leave before we had arrived for breakfast, he would have always eaten breakfast. We could tell he had not eaten breakfast that morning. As you know, I was already extremely stressed out over Pa. But not wanting to alarm anyone else yet, I said I'd go check with Pa in the fields. Then to my surprise, Bobby stood up and said, "No, I need to walk off a headache, and I will go check on Clevis."

Bobby came back about an hour later as we were cleaning up from breakfast with tears streaking down his face. We quickly understood why and all joined into gut-wrenching cries and tears ourselves. "Where is Pa?" cried all.

"Come with me" were the only words Bobby could say. The Cumberland family jumped up from the breakfast table, but Bobby asked them to remain at the campsite along with his family.

We ran quickly behind Bobby. I prayed for a miracle yet expected the worst. Bobby took us to the backside of the volcano crater deep in some trees, and there we gaped at a large wooden box made from beach flotsam and placed at the bottom of a dug hole. My father had apparently, over the course of a couple of weeks, secretly dug his own grave and constructed the box coffin, placing it at the bottom of the hole. Thankfully a top for the box with Pa inside had been firmly secured by Bobby.

My mother fainted and fell onto the box as we all screamed with our worst fear realized. "What happened?" we demanded of Bobby although we knew. Bobby explained that he'd come across the coffin with Pa leaning down against one of the trees. He took Pa's pulse, and it was too late. Bobby said he'd been fearing something like this for weeks now, as Pa had asked him to come to this spot and look for him if something strange seemed to have occurred. But since it'd been weeks since Pa's ominous request and he'd promised Pa that he wouldn't discuss his declining health with anyone else, Bobby had hoped Pa's condition had stabilized.

After about an hour of grief, Bobby thoughtfully asked us to all sit down together and let him read a letter that Pa had given to him weeks ago to only be read to his family if he ever passed on this island. Bobby explained that he believed this would answer a lot of our questions and needs at this time.

If Bobby is reading this letter to you now, then I'm with our heavenly Father. Please don't grieve for me as I'm finally home where we all will be one day. I'm with your grandparents, your uncle Jack and aunt Ruthie, and family members that had come here generations ago. Trust me, it's beautiful here and you'll never want to return to your life as you know it now. It's sort of like a baby being born who now sees a world so amazing that the warm, constantly cared for life in the mother's womb was fine at the time but couldn't compare to this birth into a wondrous world.

You're probably saying, "Why didn't he tell us he'd felt ill? We might have done something." No, you could not have done anything. You'd simply have worried, and we couldn't have enjoyed my last happy days here on the island. And no, even if we were back in Bayou La Batre, it would have been

103

my time to go. Corny, I hated so to leave you. You and I both knew my family history, and you probably could tell the last several months that I wasn't myself, but what you don't know is a confirmation that our Good Lord was getting ready for me.

Kids, I don't know whether your ma ever told you or not, but you are part Native American. It seems a long time ago your great-great-grandfather had joined the Navy and was stationed for a while in the state of Washington. It seems he was an adventuresome outdoorsman "born under a wandering star," and on one of his many adventures while stationed in Washington went fishing for salmon in the Kingcome River around Vancouver, Canada. There, the story goes that he caught a lot of fish, and more importantly, he caught a Native American for a wife, which he brought back to LA (lower Alabama). Your mother's great-great-grandmother was of the Dzawada'enuxw tribe of the Kwakwaka'wakw nation in British Columbia.

I found this out, to my surprise, when I was assigned for a short while to the Everett, Washington, military bases. The Naval Station Everett is currently the most advanced and modern military base owned and run by the United States Navy. We Marines are cousins to the Navy. I had a brief stay there at the Navy's request (there are no marine bases in Washington).

Your mother and I had only been married a short while, and I asked her to come visit me in Everett, which she did with much excitement. Shortly after arriving, I found out that I was not the only reason that she was excited to come since her great-great-ancestors had been of the First Nations village of Kingcome.

Well, I must admit that my pride was a little bruised now that I had to share your ma's glee over the trip with some American Indians, but that was okay as I have always been fascinated by these first immigrants to North America. With one of my days off, while she was here, we drove up to the Kingcome River and introduced ourselves as long-lost relatives—they welcomed us with open arms!

Amid the grandeur of the remote Pacific Northwest stands Kingcome, a village so ancient that, according to tribal myth, it was founded by the two brothers left on earth after the great flood. The Native Americans who still live there call it Quee, a place of such incredible natural richness that hunting and fishing remain primary food sources.

Several of the braves (I guess I can call them that) asked if I would accompany them on a walk in the woods where they could share some of their history and customs that only the men pass on. I know this may sound chauvinistic and even offensive, but your mother understood and agreed. Later, she explained to me that although tribal braves have their secrets and traditions, the braves treat their spouses with utmost respect, admiration, love, and kindness. They're good fathers, and they will defend their spouses to the point of death. And these are some of the most important virtues that a woman asks of a man.

The First Nations have a beautiful strength of community and a different sense of self that invites sacrifice for others. I was told by my newly found men-friends and your very distant cousins that the happiest and proudest moment in a brave's life is when their squaw (wife) presents them with a new baby, which naturally only the mother can do. And so I felt comfortable and excited about finding out some secrets and legends of Native American lore that few others knew.

We walked about a mile into a deep virgin forest along the river and stopped in the most peaceful setting I've ever seen or could imagine. We were surrounded by sequoia trees, towing one hundred feet or more; some of their diameters were over thirty feet (and I thought our live oaks were big). Boulders of huge dimensions as if tossed up by the gods enclosed our soon-built campfire. PD, you're going to love this: your father and the half dozen braves there begin smoking some type of weed. I must admit we all got a "buzz," which made it difficult for me to later recall the stories and legends that they shared with me. It may be because I was a relative, but I felt like I had the friendship of these First Nations braves. They honored me by sharing some of their deeply rooted faith and ancient beliefs.

I know you want to know what these ancient beliefs were, but my memory fades and you'll just have to do like I did and visit these wonderful Native Americans one day. For some reason, though, there was one story that stuck with me and thought about recently which I will now share:

The First Nations believe nature is endowed with spirits. As such, they pray to and ask for blessings and intercessions from nature. They believe that the forest and its inhabitants should be honored, respected, and can be called upon for assistance along with revelations about the future. One of these beliefs is that when deep and alone in the primeval forest early in the morning hours, if one hears an owl call his name, it foretells imminent death according to Kwakwaka'wakw lore.

I know this sounds crazy, but I was out in the woods the night before we left Bayou La Batre hav-

ing been awakened by that fox wreaking havoc in the chicken coop. As I ran after the fox deep into the woods with my shotgun and spotlight, suddenly, an eerie silence overcame what is usually noisy with night creatures, wind, and trees. And then softly from a distance, I did hear an owl, and it did seem to call my name!

I had forgotten about this experience back home until the First Nation shaman shared this belief with me. I know our Baptist beliefs would scoff at this, but something inside of me said, "Clevis, pay attention to this. You've been a good man. You'll always have a beautiful family that is now able to carry on without you, and you must move on to the life you were made to rise up to."

So my declining health while here on the island led me to prepare for what I believe your mother's ancestral native myth was telling me.

Corny, I could never choose *to leave you. However, somebody has been tugging at me from the next life. You have always been the love of my life, my purpose in life, my reason that I have been so happy all these years since you said yes to my proposal. I'll always remember when we first met on a blind date. You walked down the stairs from your apartment with Deanna, and my heart leaped into my throat, my mouth went dry, and I could only stutter. You were the most gorgeous girl I had ever seen, and I immediately became blindly in love. I preceded to listen to every word you spoke (does this sound familiar Parry?).*

Our Good Lord needs me now elsewhere, and our boys need you, Corny, now more than ever. One day when our Good Lord decides it's right, you'll join me again. I'll start working on our next house here soon as our Good Lord and Savior gives me the permit.

Parry, you are now head of our family, and I know you shall do well with this responsibility in addition to that of your wife and children. PD, I ask you to take over the farming activities—even though you are one of the smartest of us all, you also have a knack for farming, and I sense in you a love of it. Hopefully, you all will be rescued someday, and PD, you can return to your ultimate love of computers and the internet. Rufus, I have a feeling that you may accomplish more than all of us; I don't have a feel for what activity it will be, yet I know how you approach things with an intensity and passion yet with kindness for others that has always amazed me. You love people, and they love you back. Your peers listen to you and look to you for your leadership. You have extreme integrity and honesty. I think you have the makings of a fine politician, and that's not an oxymoron (but I do hope you don't choose politics).

To my wonderful family, you are beyond my greatest dreams, our Good Lord has blessed me with that which I am not worthy. I have always tried to do my best for you all. I hope you don't feel too ill of me as the Good Lord takes us when it's His will. He doesn't make mistakes. You all have a responsibility to carry on without me. As you kids go forward and further mature, all I ask is that you always listen to your heart, try to do the right thing, and don't worry about the outcome. The outcome is sometimes beyond our control, yet choosing the right thing to do is not. Know that I shall always love you more than life itself and will await you with open arms in a better world.

Love always,
Your husband and your father, Clevis

CHAPTER 12

Eulogy

We scheduled a service for the next day at sunup. Yes, sunup, which was Clevis's favorite time of the day. Our lives would now begin without Clevis physically with us, and our clear responsibility from this point was to live up to his expectations.

Jacob began his eulogy with, "You all know that Clevis and I had our differences. I dare say that much of the causes of our differences were our widely disparate backgrounds. That said, I must admit that I came around a lot more to Clevis's way of thinking than he came to mine, and rightfully so.

"Clevis knew I was a vain man. He knew I couldn't farm nor wanted to, yet I needed to feed my family. He came to me with the idea that I should 'manage' our needs on the island, and he'd do the farming. He knew full well that 'manage' was a minor concern here and that enabling cooperation of us all is the best I could do. But he knew this would allow me to feel and appear important.

"I might be smart, but I know Clevis was wise. He told me to always listen carefully to you, Corny, for your thoughts on how we should move forward on the island. Parry and Katelyn, Clevis asked me, as what must have been a forewarning of his time left with us, if he ever passed before we were rescued, for me to please look after the newest family on the island.

"I'm now going to address Clevis. Clevis, I only knew you a short while, yet you will remain one of my closest friends I shall ever have on this earth. I'm not in the habit of saying I'm wrong and especially to a White man. I guess a major reason is that I mistrust the typical White person addressing me more than I do with my brothers. Regardless, I was wrong about you. You have the heart which I always thought I had. You treated me and softly guided me with kindness yet stern when appropriate and coupled with genuine sincerity. I can honestly say that you are one White man completely void of any racist superiority bias which unfortunately my predilections had presupposed.

"Clevis, I shall always think of you as a brother. I shall always stand ready to help your family whenever asked or needed, as I feel you would do for mine if roles had been reversed. I welcome your son, Parry, into my family as my son. And I compliment all three of your sons in the highest manner I know of: I sense much of your father is in each of you three boys. Corny, I mean what I say, and I shall be there for you and yours as if my own.

"I would now like to share with you all one small example of many as to why I hold Clevis in highest esteem. You may or may not recall our first evening on the cruise. We were all seated at our assigned tables for dinner. The Whiteheads and the Fergusons were seated at their joint table, accommodating their nine family members along with two empty seats. For some reason, which I'm hoping had nothing to do with my family's skin color, we were seated by ourselves along with four empty places. This was a little disheartening since we always felt, in our previous cruises, that the dinner table enabled valuable socializing.

"We noticed a few tables with primarily African Americans, and so Billie was going to question the maître d' the next day why we had been alone at the table. Billie knows how curt and blunt I can be and anticipated this, thereby asserting that she would discuss it and request to be moved.

"As you know, we were moved the next day to a new table along with you Whiteheads and Fernandez families. What you don't know is what the maître d' told Billie. Before she had even made her request to be moved to a table of African Americans whom she had met that morning, the maître d' sincerely apologized for the seating miscue and stated that we would be moved that evening to a new table being prepared for us along with you two families.

"Billie asked if instead we could simply be moved to the table with the African Americans who were already delighted to have us join them. The maître d' responded, 'Oh no, please, madam, a Mr. Whitehead has already approached me and adamantly insisted that a new table be prepared for his family and the Fernandez family along with the lone family, the Cumberlands.'

"Billie tried to explain to him that it would be much easier to simply move us to the table with African Americans. But the maître d' had already spoken with Mr. Whitehead who insisted that we be moved to his table, even to the extent that he would go to the captain for his request if necessary.

"And that, my new friends, is why we ended up at your table. I must also share that my daughter Katelyn had already met Parry that morning and urged us to join you, folks. Knowing Parry like I now do, Parry may have mentioned this also to Clevis.

"You have known, and now I know, what a generous, kind-hearted, loving man Clevis Whitehead was. I'll stop now with one of the many inspirations that Clevis left me. One time I asked him how he so rarely caused contention and most often pursued harmony in our community. His simple response was, 'I strive to be kind, considerate, and useful,' and with a twinkle in his eye, added, 'and do so with a little degree of humor.' Clevis, I hope my failings will be rectified in my remaining years, or our good Lord will forgive me so that I shall see you again one day on the other side."

Bobby began with, "Clevis was my best friend. He was a painfully humble man, and so I'm going to have to tell you a few stories about this amazing man that you probably have never heard before.

"We both volunteered for the Marines during the Vietnam War in 1967. This is where we met up. We went to Parris Island for boot camp and quickly became fast friends. I was a tough kid, but not savvy like Clevis. He recognized my poor English as a handicap and took me under his wing.

"We both graduated as grunts and were sent to a battle-tested platoon at the US combat base at Khe Sanh. There it became apparent that Clevis would have serious moral and ethical problems to have to kill another human being or even hurt one. I believe this ended up causing Clevis to take up a drug habit there which he eventually brought back with him to the states.

"We weren't aware at the time that the North Vietnamese People's Army of Vietnam [PAVN] and the Vietcong [VC] were about to begin the Tet Offensive which eventually broke the back of the South Vietnamese. Our platoon engaged the PAVN/VC at the Battle of Huế where intense fighting lasted for a month, resulting in the destruction of the city. The PAVN/VC executed thousands of people in the massacre at Huế.

"The offensive was a military defeat for North Vietnam. However, this offensive had far-reaching consequences due to its effect on the views of the Vietnam War by the American public. General Westmoreland reported that defeating the PAVN/VC would require two hundred thousand more American soldiers and activation of the reserves, prompting even loyal supporters of the war to see that the current war strategy required reevaluation. The offensive had a strong effect on the US government and shocked the US public, which had been led to believe by its political and military leaders that the North Vietnamese were being defeated and incapable of launching such an ambitious military operation. American public support for the war declined as a result of the Tet casualties and the ramping up of draft calls. Subsequently, the US sought negotiations to end the war.

"During the Battle at Huế, our platoon was being decimated by enemy gunfire from a vicious machine gun in a pillbox strategically placed atop a hill. Our sergeant quickly determined that unless we took out the pillbox, the battle would be lost, and we would all likely be killed. He told me to take a load of grenades and sneak around behind the pillbox and destroy it. Clevis told the sergeant that he would go instead of me, as he was more skilled with grenades, but the sergeant, knowing that Clevis was a crack shot, told him to follow behind me and provide me fire protection as I went up the backside of the hill.

"And indeed he did provide me fire cover as I crawled up the hill. He must have taken out three or four of the enemy protecting their backside. I dropped three grenades into the pillbox, and as I leaped down the hill, they exploded, hitting me with shrapnel in my two legs. The pillbox was demolished, yet there were plenty of gooks remaining. They kept up an intense fire, pinning me down even if I could have run at that point, which I couldn't. Clevis called the sergeant to bring up several more marines to return fire. Clevis took out at least three more enemies, tossed a smoke grenade into their line of sight, and ran to me. He picked me up on his shoulders and carried me down the rest of the hill to safety as bullets whizzed by us both.

"The battle turned out to be a standoff, but our commanding officer spoke highly of the platoon's valor that day. I received the Bronze Star and a Purple Heart, and Clevis received the Navy Cross which is the second-highest award in the Marine Corps.

"He never told you this, did he? Of course not. Clevis would never tell others of this honor and made me promise not to tell his family. I asked him why, and he said he wanted his family to be proud of him as a husband and a father, and not as a soldier in a killing war unpopular back home. Well, now you know it. And, Clevis, I ask your forgiveness for telling it, but you didn't say, 'Don't ever tell.' You simply said, 'Don't tell,' and I interpreted this to mean while you were still alive.

"I want to now tell you one more story about Vietnam before the Battle of Hué. Clevis and I had been in several firefights, and it became clear to each of us in our platoon that there was a good chance maybe half of the platoon might not return home except in boxes. We were holed up in a small Vietnamese hamlet. Apparently one of the Vietnamese was a spy for us acting the part of a Vietcong and getting us intel whenever he could, often at night at grave risk to himself and his family still in the hamlet.

"One evening, we found out that the VCs would make a major assault on the hamlet knowing we were there. Our commanding officer felt like we had nowhere to go, as the VC were all around us and our support couldn't arrive for close to a week. He decided that we'd surprise them with a strong welcoming committee that they wouldn't be expecting.

"He was right, and that advanced warning by our spy probably ended up saving our lives. We held our own, taking a few casualties while the enemy were severely stricken. The main advantage that the VC had were their mortars which we had prepared for by digging fox-holes. However, the incoming mortars decimated the small hamlet.

"After the battle subsided, we went throughout the hamlet trying to save the injured. As we approached a practically demolished hut, a small boy about four years old came running out crying for his mama, clutching his dirty teddy bear. Clevis picked him up and took him to safety in the event that there were some snipers still in the area. Another survivor of the destroyed hamlet informed us that the child's surname was Nguyen, his mama had died, and his father could not be found. Clevis told the sergeant major that he'd take care of the kid which was okay with sarge as no relatives could be found nearby. Sarge figured we'd drop the kid off at the first town we came to on our rescue later that week.

"Clevis bonded with the kid, and the kid with Clevis. Days later, when it came time for us to move out, Clevis told Sarge he wanted to adopt the kid and bring him home to the US. Sarge knew this would be impossible, but seeing Clevis's unrelenting determination and even some tears in his eyes, Sarge decided to kick the can down the road, figuring those higher powers would convince Clevis that this was not possible. But nobody knew Clevis like I knew Clevis. It would indeed take higher powers and then some to separate Clevis from this four-year-old.

"And you know what, higher powers did take over. A few weeks later, as our platoon cautiously moved back to friendly environs at the next hamlet we came to, a Vietnamese came running out to meet us. It was our spy who our sergeant knew well and who had alerted us of our previous danger enabling us to prepare. However, our spy had tears in his eyes, asking, 'Why did you not remove the villagers from the hamlet?' [We couldn't because that would have given away our preparation.] 'My wife and child were killed!' he cried. We were deeply touched by his loss, and we, too, had tears in our eyes.

"Just on a whim, Clevis asked our spy what his child's last name was. He said, "Nguyen," and he was four years old. Clevis then went to his tent and brought his previously hoped-to-be adopted boy out to reunite with his real father. Understand, you're among soldiers who've killed and almost been killed. The battle-hardened marines had to wipe their eyes seeing the ecstatic reunion of father and son. Then later as we continued our pullout from this hamlet, something happened that we marines will always remember and probably with tears. As we moved out, the little boy named Nguyen ran up to Clevis and handed him his teddy bear. The tears streaming down our cheeks do not adequately portray how our hearts, at that very moment, cried out as a four-year-old child showed us what love is all about.

"My guess is that Clevis gave that teddy bear to one of you three boys."

Rufus, now with tears in his eyes, raised his hand while crying.

"Thank you, Rufus. Parry, may I ask you, what is your middle name?"

"It's Wynn."

"Do you know how *Nguyen* is pronounced? It's pronounced and sounds a lot like "Wynn."

CHAPTER 13

Eat, *Smoke*, and Be Merry

Pa was put to rest. PD and I accepted our new roles, and the islanders began adjusting to life without Pa although it would never be the same. To say we missed Pa is much too much an understatement. Our hearts felt left with a hole, and our community a ship without a rudder. Jacob recommended that we should have a GDP meeting to assess how best to move forward. The twins were getting bigger, and what had been young teenagers were now becoming young adults and seemingly spending more attention to their opposite sexes here on the island.

The GDP meeting began with Jacob suggesting that we need to plant more and fallow less. "We need to plant more food for our growing community. We should review our conveyance agreement." It seems that without Clevis's farming acumen and the fact that the reclaimed land on the beaches had produced only a fraction of the harvest on the island, our annual harvests had fallen off precipitously.

Corny interrupted with her solution. "Why don't we simply use land from each of our families' set-aside fifteen acres within the fallow plans every time newborn additions demand more farmland and forget about the need to also set aside fifteen fallow acres from each new family? This should give us plenty more years. We don't need to limit how much we can eat, or how many children we can have."

Bobby agrees and adds, "Yes, this will give us a lot of years for population growth while we're awaiting rescue. Jacob told us we'd

116

surely be rescued in no more than thirty to forty years. I've never been a big fan of so-called sustainable farming anyway. We must instead focus on the immediate needs of our families' happiness and health. After all, it's not easy living on this island."

"Excuse my profanity, GDP members. Bobby and I don't often agree on anything, but he's DAMN RIGHT HERE!" explodes Jacob. "We've suffered long enough. The conveyance method of restricting an additional fifteen acres of sanctuary land for fallow whenever our children become a new-adult family is unnecessary as is the need for today's families to maintain fifteen acres to fallow. We can just give a new family three acres to plant. My goodness, we're not going to have a Malthusian population explosion here. Any additional new families as well as present families beginning now should have no fallow requirements. Each of today's families will have their land to plant every year as each so pleases. However, we must maintain our present green space in the sanctuary for the few years until rescue. A perfect sustainable plan might possess a five-year fallow plan, but its limitations on our quality of life are impractical and punitive. We're going to get rescued soon. As I heard Clevis say, 'Don't let the perfect be the enemy of the good!'" propounds Jacob.

"Understand that to cease placing land into fallow for rejuvenation may, in the short run, increase the total harvest yields. But that is a fallacious doomsday strategy for longer term survival. This will surely come back to haunt us. Yields and quality will soon deteriorate, and the land may eventually become totally depleted and incapable of any harvest whatsoever," retorted PD. "It's analogous to our government back home in the States, having placed more and more cash into the economy while expecting wealth to increase especially for low-income Americans. Instead, after doing so, what descended on America was continued hyperinflation and devaluation of the dollar, actually harming those it was touted to help. It's how a brief temporary gain in our harvest from terminating our fallow requirement will eventually reverse and lower yields, damaging our welfare to intolerable levels."

"PD, you said that increased inflation and devaluation of the dollar could be especially harmful to low-income Americans. Why could it be more harmful to low-income than upper-income?" a confused Jesse asked.

"High inflation, which occurs across the board, affects those regular everyday expenses that we all need to live, such as food, gasoline, utility expenses, rent, taxes, etc., regardless of whether we are low-income or upper-income Americans. However, low-income Americans have a much larger proportion coming out of their income to cover regular everyday expenses than do upper-income Americans. [You can think of what is left over from income after paying regular everyday expenses as what will be available for savings, investments, or longer-term expenses.] Imagine that low-income Americans have 90 percent of income as everyday expenses while the proportion for upper-income Americans is 40 percent. Let's assume that income for neither low-income nor upper-income Americans increases with inflation [this is probably truer for low-income than upper-income Americans during times of high inflation, but we'll assume the same effect for both to make the example more straightforward; we'll also *ignore* the fact that what's left over, such as investments, savings, and longer-term expenses, probably keeps up better with inflation for upper-income Americans than does it for low-income Americans in order to continue to make the example simple.] If general inflation is high, it will not take long before low-income families have a deficit with their income to cover regular everyday expenses while high-income Americans will still be able to adequately cover their regular everyday expenses," explained PD.

"PD is right. We need to live within our means today and with a sustainable methodology. We've done a good job of converting the breadfruit into an edible paste for storage years into the future which should enable consumption in the event of a devasting harvest. However, lately, even with our current fallow methodology, it seems that we've been eating somewhat into this safety supply and failing to restore it. We can't continue this. I know sacrifice is unwelcome anytime, yet sacrifice now can lead to replenished reserves tomorrow or even mere survival," I cautioned.

"As PD said and I must stress," asserted Karma, "We all remember the calamity our American government got us into after the economic downturn created by the coronavirus in which the Feds flooded the economy with greenbacks. Recall how this led to unsustainable inflation along with debt and interest payments that were greater than the gross national product [total market value of goods and services produced by all citizens and capital], endangering the capability of the country to pay its annual debt and consequently eating into its assets like we've been recently eating into our stored food [breadfruit paste]. We may already be on a dangerous path of *creeping normalcy*," Karma cried.

"What in the world do you mean by that?" begged Corny.

"It can be a process by which a major change [and in this case, a negative change] becomes accepted as normal and acceptable if it happens slowly through small, often unnoticeable, increments of change such as growth in a population. For instance, eventually we young adults, unless rescued, hope to wed like Parry and Katelyn, and then have children of our own," responded Karma.

"*Creeping normalcy* sounds a lot like the expression *death by a thousand cuts*," chuckled PD.

Nonetheless, several members began agreeing with Corny and Bobby's idea of thinking surely rescue will occur over the next few years. Rufus, however, is dumbfounded. "And what'll happen if all the acres of arable land on the entire island are planted with no additional acreage in fallow while using only Parry and me to help PD? Are we stupid or just nearsighted? Have we stayed too long on the beach in the sun?

"You're creating an environment that will result in an irreversible deficit [i.e., the inability to grow enough food and eating into our stored breadfruit paste at a higher and unsustainable rate than we had originally anticipated when setting up the plan for storing paste during years of plenty]. With our loss of arable, fertile land as we abandon fallow, you will effectively be digging a hole which neither we nor our children will be able to climb out. You're effectively creating a debt by excess consumption and future declining harvest yields which cannot be repaid tomorrow! It's a doomsday deficit that will end up requiring extreme suffering for all unless there's rescue or divine intervention. Didn't you hear Mr. Cumberland talk about the collapse of Easter Island? We must maintain a sustainable environment since we don't know how long we or our descendants will be here. Do you want us or our descendants to end up as starving cannibals?"

"Why must you be so pessimistic? We can't let today always suffer for what might happen in the future," argues Missy.

"Okay, we've heard your counter concern, Rufus," Jacob interjected. "I'm impressed that you listened so earnestly to my story of Easter Island, but the outside world didn't even know then where Easter Island was, let alone the fact that some natives had landed there. The outside world knows we were on that cruise ship and were abandoned on an island somewhere along the route to Australia. They will surely discover us way before we've run out of useful acreage and timber.

"Listen, I hate to use up *green-space*, which is our sanctuary, more than anyone, but we must use it if necessary in the future. But we mustn't let our quality of life be diminished. We've sacrificed enough already. Also, if that *fat chance event* of running out of acreage were to happen, we'll merely continue to place barriers into the shallow water on the beach and create even more land to farm, like the Japanese have been doing for generations."

"I'm glad you mentioned the Japanese, Mr. Cumberland," added Karma. "You're right. They have existed for thousands of years on a few relatively small islands with limited arable land. One-fifth of the islands are opportune for its people and agriculture. Today it has the highest population density of any first-world country. However, one of the ways it has so managed to exist and prosper is forest, land, and agriculture management. Their forest management was coupled with less use of wood.

"Plus, another important possible lesson for us is that the Japanese have achieved almost zero-population growth over the years. For example, from 1721 to 1828, Japan's population increased from twenty-one million to only twenty-seven million. Individual couples helped decrease birth rates when observing perceived shortages of food and other resources. I don't want to limit our population growth, and therefore, I strongly believe we must continue our practice of sustainable fallow practices."

"Yes, I agree," I added. "Also, I'd like to add regarding reclaimed land from the beaches to exist indefinitely if we were never rescued, what if another storm comes along and destroys this reclaimed land from the beaches? And the current farmed land will have diminishing annual harvesting if we abandon Clevis's recommended fallow requirements. Mr. Cumberland, while I do understand your point about the differences in Easter Island and us, I must agree with Rufus. We've been here for a considerable number of years, and the outside world may think we're dead since we were infected with coronavirus when we were left here," I cautioned. "We should operate under the premise that there will be no rescue."

"Okay, what we have here is a mind-bending conundrum. We've had enough discussion. Before we limit pregnancy, reduce food consumption, and make life here ever more difficult than it already is, we must have a vote," demands Jacob. "All in favor of modifying our conveyance plan as outlined by Corny and Bobby, say yes. All opposed, say no."

Yes—Jacob
Yes—Katelyn
Yes—Bobby
Yes—Maria
Yes—Jesse
No—Karma
No—Billie
Yes—Corny
No—Rufus
No—PD
No—Parry
Yes—Missy

"Since Clovis and Venus are too young to vote, the yeses have it seven to five," Jacob announces. "The majority has spoken. Our plan will be amended as described by Corny and Bobby."

"Wait a minute, Mr. Cumberland," I interrupted. "I must stress how extremely disappointed I am with the vote. I know democracy rules and that it is the best of all governing systems man has ever devised, yet it can be wrong. Remember what Rick Warren said, that an untruth is not a truth, a wrong become a right, nor a mistake become a solution just because it is approved in a vote or simply accepted by a majority.

"We in the United States consider our wisest, most objective body to be our Supreme Court. Ma, do you know that in Roe versus Wade in 1973, not only did our Supreme Court rule via a majority vote that unborn children implicitly have no legal rights, but they did so rule while ignoring the fact that abortion as constitutional right does not appear to have any basis in text, structure, history, or traditions [i.e., how is abortion even a constitutional issue?].

"Mr. Cumberland, my guess is that you're aware that in *Plessy versus Ferguson*, our Supreme Court voted in favor of *separate but equal* treatment for the races. This mistake in judgement was later corrected in the 1964 Civil Rights Act.

"Bobby, did you know that on December 8, 1944, by a vote of 6–3, our Supreme Court ruled that an *American citizen* could be placed into an internment camp because of his Japanese ancestry and that these Japanese Americans were so placed until near the end of WWII?

"I point out these mistakes in majority voting, later corrected, not to be so arrogant, vain, or even naive as to assert that I and the minority on this vote as to whether to continue fallow practices is right and that the majority is therefore wrong. I say this simply to ask the majority to think deeply about what they are about to do and the future impacts it will have on all of us. We may not be able later to correct ourselves."

And just like that, we discarded any thoughts or concerns for sustainability and management of our resources. We effectively threw our capabilities to control our destiny away and left ourselves susceptible to the vagaries of an unfettered future. I was reminded of our country which I love, but had discarded budgetary limitations, planning, and control by resorting to the simple act of allowing unrestricted printing of money to address today's appetites without regard for the deficit and future economic consequences.

"Any further business?" asked Jacob.

"I propose we place a note in one of our remaining bottles that were left after we landed. We'll demand to know, 'Where is our rescue?'" sarcastically laughed Missy. "We'll explain everything that has happened to us as best we can and toss that sucker into the Pacific. Maybe someone will find it, realize we're still here, and renew the search."

The meeting is adjourned, and the GDP members rose to return to their daily activities, except for a few voters—Missy and Rufus—who decide to simply chill out with PD and his *weed* on the beach.

The End

*****

"Why did you end the story of the islanders, Beebop?" questioned Lila.

"The messages in the bottles quit coming."

EPILOGUE

The initial draft of this story was written about ten years ago. Afterward, another message in a bottle washed up on the shore of La Jolla, California.

Katelyn and Parry had become the proud parents of two boys and two girls. PD and Missy had tied the proverbial knot and have three of their own with a fourth *bun in the oven*. Rufus and Karma are, for all practical purposes, married although not officially married. They just wanted to live together, much to the dismay of their parents. Rufus and Karma have two children. The island population is now five senior adults, seven young adults, and nine children; evidently there's not a whole lot else to do on a deserted island.

A terse message in a recently found bottle concluded with the following demand:

> *We islanders—Cumberlands, Fernandez, and Whiteheads—are still living our lives on this remote island. Recently, a container from an ocean-going container ship washed up on our island shores. Apparently, it had fallen off the container ship during a storm at sea. With much difficulty, we opened the refrigerated container and found a load of partially thawed frozen chicken possibly bound for Asia from the West Coast. Until it began spoiling, the chicken made for several scrumptious barbecues for which we are most appreciative.*

*We also found a US newspaper inside the con-
tainer. (Lord only knows why there was a newspaper in the container—maybe whoever was loading
it decided to take a break and read about Jacob's
team, the Warriors.) The month-old newspaper gave
us a pretty good idea of what has happened in the
US over the past fifteen to twenty years that we have
lived on our island (we have no way of keeping track
of years here as even a Rolex can malfunction).*

*The newspaper indicates that the US dollar
currency has started to crumble due to continued
hyperinflation. Consumer spending power has
apparently been crushed damaged by inadequate
salaries. Livelihood and family wealth is declining.
It seems the government is strapped for sufficient
cash. Subsidies are being withdrawn, creating isolated, exorbitant price spikes. The government is
seriously considering controlling the prices of selected
medications. Many middle-income families may
be pushed into lower-income or even poverty. Some
skilled workers are leaving the country.*

*At a GDP meeting, we discussed, and all
agreed how alarmed and distressed we are with the
apparent and frightful changes that have occurred
in the US during our absence. So much so that we
therefore strongly request that you—DESTROY ANY
PRIOR MESSAGES FROM OUR BOTTLES AND DISCON-
TINUE ANY RESCUE EFFORTS ON OUR BEHALF.*

With twenty-one mouths to feed indefinitely, evidently the
islanders have wisely discarded their amendment that would have
required them to cease fallow requirements. This must have thereby
prevented any catastrophic consequences. These people were apparently able to withstand and adjust to despair, adversity, and dire circumstances. They must have learned how to sustain, maintain, and
prosper both physically and emotionally. Each one somehow found a

meaning for their life. There is no way to predict how long they will be able to do so.

Huge civilizations have survived for hundreds of years: Rome survived for 500 years; the Ming Dynasty lasted over 275 years; the Ottomans over 450 years; and the British Empire about 350 years. There are numerous reasons why these great dynasties eventually fell or diminished: they may have lost sight of a purpose or meaning for what had sustained them; they may have not been able to live indefinitely with prosperity, wealth inequity, or they simply became lazy. A creeping normalcy may have occurred such as gradual excess living for today with promises to pay back tomorrow could have ultimately caused their demise.

I fear today for our great country tomorrow.

APPENDIX

Message to the Reader

Now, you've read this story about marooned islanders and their limited resources. I hope you understand this metaphor for our country's deficit spending.

Our country has added trillions of dollars to our national debt after the coronavirus, the economic stimulus, and the "infrastructure" bill. Can we create a plan to do something about our national debt danger, or just trust in providence and a rescue ship?

Apparently, our islanders have survived for about twenty-some-odd years. The Easter Islanders flourished for a while. Will our islanders experience an unsustainable tipping point? Will our islanders end up as simply another Easter Island?

We can understand how farming more and more of the island's finite land and the use of reclaimed beaches can increase total food harvest to satisfy demand—*for a while*. Then eventual harvest declines begin occurring to harm our islanders. Similarly, how long can our country keep flooding the economy with money to satisfy its excess *wants* which it can do through buying up bonds or simply printing dollars exacerbating inflation and harming those the plan was meant to help? Hyperinflation (waiting in the weeds) severely harms the middle- and lower-income classes much more so than the upper-income class.

The marooned islanders' population growth and eating habits coupled with increasing use of land without fallow planning even with the use of reclaimed beach land is like expecting an increasingly exorbitant money supply to have sustainable value and reasonable inflation in the future, but can it? Can productivity and output be able to keep pace with demand? Expecting reclaimed sand on the beach to have output similar to the island land is like printing new money in hopes of expanding commensurate productivity and output indefinitely; there's little value for reclaimed sand nor newly printed money, as seen in our growing national debt.

Will America reach a tipping point? Will we be able to continue indefinitely paying for our growing debt? Will our future be beset with runaway inflation? Inflation can prevent what would have been productivity gains and innovation.

What exactly will happen to our country if we continue simply increasing our national debt without limits? Will it be easier for our children's future society sometime in the future to pay back this debt? Many wise economists say it will not. Will future Americans be able to survive this inevitable crisis? The Scottish philosopher Alexander Tyler of the University of Edinburgh details eight stages to the rise and fall of the world's greatest civilizations, and we are often considered history's best of civilizations. We have experienced the first four of Mr. Tyler's stages and have arrived at the fifth stage: abundance. These final four are our country's challenges:

> Stage 5 is a movement from abundance to complacency. Society, in general, becomes self-satisfied and increasingly unaware of serious trends that undermine health and the ability to thrive. Foundations, resources, infrastructures, and necessary virtues are deteriorating. Those who try to alarm the masses are shouted down by the complacent.
>
> Stage 6 is a change from complacency to apathy. Citizens fail to remember or refuse to consider the sacrifices and suffering of previous generations and are willing to live on the car-

casses of their fathers and mothers. Hard work and self-discipline erode.

Stage 7 moves from apathy to dependence. The increasing numbers who lack virtue and the desire to work and contribute become dependent upon a governmental handout. Discipline and work are "too hard," and dependence grows. The bulk of society considers sacrifice and suffering as intolerable. "Others must solve the needs of the masses."

Stage 8, the final stage, is the change from dependence to bondage, as the government has become a huge centralized power and ultimate caretaker in the minds of the multitudes. Dependent citizens become dysfunctional and desperate. Those in bondage know of no other solution than the centralized government. Family and personal virtues, creativity, and individual ambition have been replaced by the despotic centralized government, ever hungry for more power over the masses. And since individuals are the real creators and producers of wealth and abundance, not the government, we find that few such nations last much more than several hundred years.

Our country is almost two hundred and fifty years old. Are we declining as a people? Are we experiencing *creeping normalcy* disintegration? It is up to us, as it was up to the islanders, to control our future or be controlled by it.

I was asked if the story would have a happy ending. You decide.

ABOUT THE AUTHOR

Michael Thomas O'Sheasy was born April 15, 1948, at St. Francis Hospital in Charleston, South Carolina. He was raised on James Island, an island overlooking the Charleston harbor and north of Kiawah Island. It is home to two strategic forts: Fort Johnson during the Revolutionary War and Fort Pemberton during the Civil War. Mr. O'Sheasy received an engineering degree in 1970 from Georgia Institute of Technology and an MBA in 1974 from Georgia State University.

Mr. O'Sheasy spent most of his career in the electricity industry with the Southern Company serving as an expert in costing and pricing. He created many innovative pricing products which are still in use throughout the industry. Mr. O'Sheasy was an expert witness in these fields, testifying as a consultant on behalf of utilities throughout North America and the Caribbean. His consulting work also included electric utilities in Europe and Asia.

Mr. O'Sheasy has been married to Susan for over fifty years and now lives on a lake north of Atlanta, Georgia. He has two daughters—Beth and Caroline—and four grandchildren: Caleb, Lila, Ethan, and Dylan.

CPSIA information can be obtained
at www.ICGtesting.com
Printed in the USA
BVHW041230090623
665685BV00016B/557/J

9 781639 619955